AN EVERGLADES ROMANCE

Chapter 1

Bands of yellow haze were smeared across the sky to the far horizon. Nicole Carpenter had been hoping to catch a clear view of the Everglades as the small plan descended. She leaned back in her seat and sighed. So much had changed in just a few months, and none of it seemed like it was for the better.

She raised a pale hand to the pendant strung on a silver chain around her neck, and slowly smoothed the blue-green stone between her thumb and forefinger like a worry bead. The orb, carved from an azurite- malachite cluster, resembled a miniature planet earth. The necklace had been a gift from her parents when she had finished her first semester of art school. A now-familiar sadness rose in her heart. Maybe moving down to Naples, Florida so soon hadn't been such a good idea.

She turned back to the book on her lap, *Bird Behavior,* and opened it to the marked page, determined to refocus her attention on the text describing a close-up photograph of six large birds competing for space on a tree limb.

"Lovely, aren't they?"

Nicole was a little startled by the question, and quickly looked back down at the picture. "Yes. They are."

"Yellow-crowned night herons. Ever seen an old oak tree with bunches of them perched on every branch, squabbling with each other for prime real estate?"

Nicole looked over at the elderly man strapped into the seat next to her. His smile was reassuring.

"No. No, I haven't." Nicole smiled back at him, encouraged by his calm, friendly demeanor.

"Well, then, you ought to. And the best place to check them out would be in the Everglades. In fact, it's the best place to see 'most any of the southern birds or the northern visitors.

"I've never visited the Everglades," Nicole confessed, "although I would like to."

"'Visit' them?" the old man laughed, not unpleasantly. "Well, they're not very much like Disney World, you know. You don't buy a ticket and take a day trip. You really have to spend some time learning to understand the attractions of the land. A quick drive or an air boat tour out to watch some semi-tame alligators being fed supermarket chicken won't really help. A quick tour on your way to Miami or Naples won't do at all.

Nicole smiled. "I just might be taking your advice before long. I have an aunt who runs a bed and breakfast off Highway 41, and she's been persistent in her invitations. I've been so busy I haven't had a chance, but I'm considering packing up my mosquito repellent and driving out there one of these days, now that I'm living so much closer."

"Good for you!" The old man seemed quite delighted at the idea. "Be sure to bring your bird book. You'll see some wonderful specimens you'll want to identify." The smile left his face, and he looked sad. "You should go while there's still time. The Everglades are disappearing, acre by acre."

Nicole turned once more to look out the small window at her left. The old man noticed the direction of her gaze. "See that smoke out there?" Nicole nodded. "Fires. The 'Glades are on fire. Apparently some fool must have left a campfire burning, or some such criminal stupidity, and now we're losing some more of our precious wildlife. Saddens me to think of it." He sighed deeply, trying to gain control of his emotions.

"Of course, part of it is just how Mother Nature seems to work," he went on. "Some years, there's enough rain. Some years, there's too much rain, and that can be a problem. And some years, like this one, there's not enough. I sure hope it doesn't turn out to be as bad as that awful drought we had way back in 1971. All that muck out there, when it gets dry, it burns like peat."

Just then, the small plane began to bounce as it hit a series of air pockets. Nicole's eyes darkened with anxiety, and her knuckles turned white as she gripped the armrests.

"You can relax," her companion soothed. "We'll be down soon. Just a little typical atmospheric turbulence."

Nicole swallowed, and clasped her hands.

"I've come to fear flying," she confessed. "I would have preferred to drive down from Orlando, but I was afraid my car couldn't have made it. The transmission's being overhauled," she explained. "I was hoping for a calmer flight."

"Do you have family here in Florida?" the man inquired, trying to take her mind off the flying.

"Just my aunt, now. The one who wants me to come out to visit, out in the Everglades."

"I'm pretty much alone, myself," said the man. "John Martin's the name. I'm in pharmaceuticals. My wife died two years ago, and I try to keep myself busy by going on the road for the company. The traveling helps."

Nicole turned her head away, so he wouldn't see her lovely brown eyes fill with tears. She was recalling the last time she had ever seen her mom and dad alive.

Nicole had arranged a garden party in celebration of their twenty-fifth wedding anniversary at their comfortable home in Clearwater. Islands of double-blossomed hibiscus, bright yellow allamandas, and the beautiful Tropicana and Queen Elizabeth rose bushes, which had been Mrs. Carpenter's pride and joy, were lending scent and color to the festivities.

She remembered watching her mom and dad hold hands and smile, their love for each other shining from their faces, as they, in turn watched their guests enjoy themselves around the pool. When people came up to them and offered congratulations for having managed to remain married for so long, they had shaken off the comments, responding that the years had been a privilege and a joy to share, certainly not some kind of hurtle to have overcome.

Now they were dead, killed in the crash of a small commuter plane. Nicole still couldn't truly accept it, even though she had driven up to Clearwater from Sarasota to handle the funeral arrangements herself until other relatives had rushed in from California and Wisconsin. She found herself expecting it to be her mother calling when her cell phone rang on a Sunday afternoon, and it hurt not to be able to share the details of her problems and her successes with her dad.

More than anyone, they had encouraged Nicole to do something with er artistic talents. They had been thrilled when she had applied and been accepted to the art school in Sarasota. No one applauded her graduation exhibit more enthusiastically, and their sympathetic shoulders were always waiting when she felt the need for some support during the rigorous, exhilarating months she had spent learning skills to express her vision of the world on canvas and rag paper and in potters' clay. Now that they were gone, Nicole was alone in the world.

As her plane decelerated down the runway at the Naples airport, Nicole shook off some of her gloomy mood. She reminded herself that she had been very fortunate to have been hired at the Pelican Gallery so soon after completing her art classes in Sarasota.

The job interview last month had been fun. Allen Davies, the English-born owner, had been pleased that she had both a business and an art background. He had quickly hired her after a check of her excellent references, and had even helped her to find a place to live in Naples within walking distance of the gallery.

Nicole's apartment building had white stucco walls and a red barrel-tiled roof. It was part of an old Spanish-style estate from the 1920's that had been converted into apartments. She didn't mind that her corner unit was small. It had gorgeous hardwood floors, high ceilings, and tall windows facing north and east. Outside grew coconut palms, and the courtyard was filled with the colorful blossoms of tropical plants. She loved the scent of the pink and purple bougainvillea wafting up through the open windows of her bedroom, and was soothed to sleep at night by the gentle rustling of long, graceful palm fronds that reflected the silver of the moonlight.

After having said a warm farewell to John Martin at the airport, Nicole found her way home by taxi. When she arrived at her apartment, the first thing she did after turning on the air conditioning wan her ceiling fan was to sit down and open her mail. She was nearly though reading a newsy, cheerful letter from her Aunt Jane when her cell phone buzzed.

"Hello, ducks!" Allen greeted her. "So glad you arrived back safely. Did you run into any trouble?"

"Everything went perfectly, Allen. I took good care of your business up in Orlando, and now I'm back unscathed, as they say."

"Who's the 'they'? Allen chuckled. "Not so much we English."

"Well, you English have enough peculiar expressions of your own, I'd say. By the way, how's my little car doing?"

"It runs beautifully, how. I went down to the shop just this afternoon and took it for a test ride. It's ready whenever you want me to deliver it." He paused. "Did you manage to pick up my package all right?"

"Of course I did, Allen, "replied Nicole. "After all, it was only one hundred percent of the reason I was there," she joked. "Your personal courier service. I'll bring it in to work tomorrow."

Allen cleared his throat. "Would it be terribly intrusive if I came 'round to pick it up today? I've been concerned about it, perhaps more than I should be. Would in an hour be convenient?"

"Well, okay, I guess so," replied Nicole with a shrug of her shoulders. What's the big rush? she wondered.

****

It was late afternoon before the swamp fire just west of the Big Cypress Seminole Indian Reservation was contained. Ren Steele sat on a tree stump. He pushed back a lock of black hair that had tumbled down over his thick eyebrows. The whites of his blue eyes were still red and irritated from the smoke. His damp shirt clung to his back. Lenny, another of the volunteers who had given precious assistance in containing the fire, handed Ren a cold beer. They all sat quietly for a time, surveying the vast, smoldering acreage.

"You don't want to know what I'd like to do to whoever started this fire," said one of the men.

"At this point, I'd vote for a lynching, except I'm too tired," said a younger man as he tried to wipe off some of the soot from his face with a filthy handkerchief.

"Is it clear that a person even started it/ Couldn't it have been set off by lightning?" inquired another.

"What lightning? There hasn't been any electrical storms in ages. Nope, it's careless people this time. Camp fires. Tossed cigarette butts".

"We ought to call them 'couldn't care less' people," retorted Lenny. "They don't care about Big Cypress, or the wildlife, or about what we have to go through out here fighting their fires."

"They care about wild life," joked another if the sweaty, sooty men. "The kind they go stalking over in Miami Beach when they finally get off Alligator Alley."

Ren Steele stood up and stretched his lean, six-foot body. He turned back to Lenny. "I wonder how that fawn we pulled out of that burning hammock is doing."

"His leg seems okay," Lenny replied. "Just got caught in some roots, I guess, running from the fire. Probably panicked and lost his footing. I'll keep him with me tonight, and turn him loose father south tomorrow. I'm going down to Everglades City, anyway."

"I'm going to get going, then," said Ren. "I've got to be over in Naples before dark."

"When will you be back out this way?" inquired Lenny.

"Over the weekend, most likely. Possibly sooner. I'll be working on the camp. I'll find you and we can get together."

"Sounds good," Lenny called after the retreating figure of Ren Steele. He turned to the others. "That's a pretty decent fellow, even if he is basically a city dude."

"What is someone like that doing out here in the swamp?"

"Must like it, I guess," Lenny shrugged. "His grandfather owned a whole lot of farmland near Lake Okeechobee back in the fifties. Used to grow sugar cane. Ever since the last big drought, though, I hear that Steele's just let all that acreage go. Won't farm it, won't hunt on it, and won't sell it."

"What's he do for his living, then?"

Lenny shrugged again. "They say he already did what he needed to do back when he was really young. Acquired land up near Orlando that the Disney people eventually wanted."

"He don't live like he's rich. That place of his by Everglades City isn't so much better than anyone else's."

"No," Lenny admitted. "I guess he just loves it here, same as us."

"Well," snorted the other man, "Love is one thing, but I can tell you that if I had money, I wouldn't waste any time at all getting out of this swamp. I'd head right for Miami, and I wouldn't stop living it up until my liver couldn't take it any more." He took a final slug of his drink and tossed the empty can into the back of his pick-up truck. "Well, I've got to get home to the wife. Let's do this again some time."

The tired men laughed, and began to load their equipment and their exhausted bodies into their vehicles. The younger man looked a the sky.

"Maybe we won't have to worry more this season. Sure looks like some serious rain to me. I hope."

Lenny backed his truck out onto the dirt access road. "it can rain all it wants, as far as I'm concerned. In fact, I wouldn't raise a complaint if it rained every day for the next month. The drought's been killing so far this season."

****

Nicole found herself pacing nervously as she waited for Allen's arrival. Her daily routine had been upset by the trip to Orlando, and she was still a little undone by the flying. Her palms were damp with a bit of anxiety as she anticipated Allen's knock at her door. Allen was infectiously cheerful, and very kind to her, but something seemed to be slightly awkward when they were together. She supposed it would take time for her to get over her parents' deaths and feel ready for a relationship with a man.

Nicole sighed and sat down on her sunny-colored apricot sofa and leaned back against the soft, plump cushions. She brushed back a strand of her silky chestnut hair and picked up the letter from her aunt. Beginning to read from where she'd left off, it became clear that her aunt was fed up with Nicole's excuses for delaying a visit to her tourist lodge.

Aunt Jane, an active, outdoorsy woman in her early fifties, was Nicole's mother's older sister. Her husband had died a few years earlier, leaving Aunt Jane alone, as they had no children. Never one to be slowed down by a problem or a challenge, she had taken all of her savings and invested them with a business partner, Fred, in a small guest house operation at the edge of the Everglades.

Advertising her business as a rustic lodge with a focus on ecotourism, she had soon developed a regular clientele of wildlife lovers from as far north as Ontario. She acquired a fleet of air boats and skiffs, and hired local guides to provide nature tours into areas of the great swamp inaccessible by other means. While there were other, similar operations, her business was unique on its strict focus on education and preservation of South Florida's wildlife and habitat. As a result, it was not uncommon for well-know photographers, artists and writers to show up at the lodge.

One of her very first guests had been the editor of a national wildlife foundation's publication. It had been his suggestion that she stock some art supplies and photography accessories for sale to guests. This had proven to be a smart business decision, as the nearest town selling such items was Naples. He had also written an article about travel to the Everglades, and had mentioned favorably "a certain little rustic establishment catering to the serious wildlife-lover or nature artist". After that story appeared in print, business was usually quite good at the Cypress Retreat, as it came to be called.

Nicole was smiling again when she had finished her aunt's letter, and resolved to reply saying that she would love to come for a few days as soon as she could get some time off from her gallery job. Aunt Jane's cheerful determination to make the best of situations certainly seemed to work out well for her. It would be wonderful to spend some time there, and to go out into the hammocks to do some painting and to feel closer to nature. There was so much she wanted to forget…

A rap at her door rescued Nicole from any further descent into gloomy thoughts. Allen Davies tap danced his way into the apartment with a big smile and whirled Nicole around before kissing her warmly on the cheek.

"I hope you're not too tired to see me, but I couldn't wait to welcome you back." Allen grinned impishly, and Nicole began to smile, too.

"Would the lady care to accompany me outside to view her very own carriage? All its horses are running quite spiritedly."

"Oh, Allen, I never expected you to drop it off! Thank you so much!"

"Personal service for a very special lady" Allen bowed as if to royalty.

"Don't let me forget, I have something for you, too." She went into her bedroom and returned with the wrapped package she had picked up for Allen. Allen set it down and took Nicole by the hand.

"Where shall we go for dinner tonight, oh my most-valued of employees? Name it, and we shall dine most sumptuously," he went on in his playful courtier mode. "But, I'm afraid we shall have to take your carriage, as I couldn't quite manage to drive both mine and yours over at the same time, and it seems all my footmen were otherwise occupied."

Nicole smiled. Allen was such good company, and he was a wonderful boss at the gallery. He was full of good humor, and went out of his way to build up Nicole's spirits when she seemed a little low. He had taught her much about the gallery's business operations, and demonstrated his confidence in her by frequently leaving her in charge while he attended to his dealings elsewhere. Allen encouraged Nicole's own talent in art, and had promised her a showing of her work a the gallery whenever she felt ready. He never pushed her into anything, but instead helped her to feel confidence in her abilities to take on new projects.

At the pleasant beach-side seafood restaurant, they dined on fresh yellow-tail snapper from the Gulf of Mexico. Nicole ordered hers broiled, with rice and a tomato and artichoke heart salad on the side. Allen ordered his fish Cajun-style.

"They really mean it when they say "blackened", don't they?" he quipped when his plate of decidedly crisp-looking fish arrived.

"They really mean it when they say 'hot', too," Nicole warned.

"I'm almost too frightened to try this," he joked. "And you Yanks have the nerve to critique nice, wholesome English dishes like blood pudding."

Allen kept the conversation pleasant and low-key, and Nicole soon found herself feeling more relaxed than she had in several days. She confided in Allen that being with him made her feel warm and cared for, the way she felt reading her aunt's letter.

Allen grimaced a bit at the comparison, but listened attentively as Nicole described what her aunt had said about her lodge in the Everglades. He took hand and squeezed it. "I can see what it would mean to you to go for a visit. Why not take a few days' holiday, and drive out?"

"Allen, you're very kind," Nicole said firmly "but I've just been up to Orlando. I couldn't possibly go off again right away."

"You did me a great favor by picking up my package personally. It saved me a good deal of worry about it arriving safely. Business at the gallery is a little slow right now. You want to go. Now would be a good time. It's as simple as that." He smiled impishly. "And when you return, you will be all refreshed and ready to work very hard on some new promotions I'm thinking about."

Nicole felt herself tearing up with gratitude, which turned her hazel eyes a deep green. "Thank you so much," she said with heart-felt sincerity. "You're the best friend I have right now. I don't know how I'd manage without you."

"I hope we get around to changing that some day soon," Allen said a bit grumpily. "I may want to be something more than just your 'good friend' someday." He put an arm across the back of her chair and smiled at her warmly.

A cellist and a violinist played a lovely, haunting melody. Nicole hummed a snatch of the lilting air, and she closed her eyes. Her life in Naples held promise. The waiter came over for their dessert order, startling Nicole out of her reverie. She opened her eyes and looked around. Allen smiled. "Only happy thoughts, I hope?"

Nicole nodded, but her smile quickly faded. Her eyes were locked on a couple who had just strolled in to the dining room behind a most deferential maitre d'. The woman was blond and svelte, dressed in a clinging white dress accessorized only by her stunning curves and her rich tan. The man was tall and dark, with bold features and piercing blue eyes. Nicole swallowed, her mouth suddenly gone dry.

As he escorted his companion to their choice table near an atrium, the man's eyes found Nicole's face across the crowded room. They blazed sapphire for an instant, registering surprise and something else that made Nicole shiver. Nicole felt pinned to her seat by his stare, and her breath caught in her throat.

Ren Steele was the last person she had expected to see. It was only when he had finally turned away to seat his companion with an easy grace that Nicole remembered to breathe again. Color suffused her face and decollete, and she turned to Allen in a state of near-panic.

"I don't feel well. Please excuse me." She got up from her seat and rushed blindly from the dining room. Allen studied the seated couple thoughtfully before he rose and followed Nicole out of the restaurant.

Chapter 2

Nicole lay flattened on her bed feeling miserable and humiliated. She could not seem to stop the images that kept flickering in her mind in an endless, repeating loop of the episode at the restaurant.

She felt sure that her stammered excuses to Allen had left him more confused than satisfied, although he had shown her nothing but concerned attention since they had careened out of the parking lot of the restaurant, Nicole at the wheel of her car.

He had talked her into letting him take over the driving after a few blocks. Nicole had realized that her behavior was appearing more irrational than ill, and she desperately wanted to avoid any need for explanations. It had taken almost a half hour back at her apartment for Allen to become convinced that she was not so seriously ill as to require the services of a doctor. Her relief was enormous when Allen had finally left, after calling a cab and promising to check in on her the first thing in the morning.

Despite feeling guilty for having allowed Allen to continue to worry that she might really be sick, Nicole simply could not bring herself to explain her abrupt change

in behavior at the restaurant. She did not want him or anyone to know what she had discovered there tonight with such painful clarity: that her feelings for Ren Steele were
still as powerful and confused as they had been on that first warm, lush night.

It had begun not long after Nicole had started her work at the Pelican. Allen was hosting an evening party on the gallery floor to mark the opening of an exhibit of watercolors by a new artist of great promise. The artist produced lovely, ethereal beach scapes, giving shimmering life to coastal scenes. Nicole had been thrilled when Allen had asked her to act as his hostess at the opening. It would be a marvelous way to become acquainted with some of the local talent and patrons in the area, which could be helpful in her work at the gallery.

Nicole had enjoyed herself very much at the party. She had dressed in a becoming coral silk shift that flattered her lightly tanned skin. Her duties as hostess were simple and pleasant. She greeted newcomers as they arrived, and introduced them to other guests she thought they might like to get to know. She kept the trays of hors d'oeuvres filled and the wine flowing. In no time at all, the two or three dozen people present were mingling on their own, talking about the watercolors on exhibit, and Nicole had relaxed. Then, Ren Steele had stepped across the threshold.

He was wearing a tuxedo that fit his lean, muscled frame as if it had been custom-tailored. His chiseled features held a mildly sardonic expression, but his blue eyes weren't unfriendly. He slowly worked his way across the room toward Nicole. She stood frozen, watching him and unable to comprehend why she felt she could not move or speak as long as his eyes held hers. He moved closer and she became aware of the smooth, male scent of his aftershave and of the broad expanse of his shoulders under his jacket. Her cheeks flushed scarlet and, embarrassed by her response to this stranger, she had stammered a humiliatingly trite comment and fled through the open French doors to the patio bar.

Allen was there to offer her a glass of wine and a canape'. Nicole accepted them with a flutter of hands and a distracted smile. She felt sure that Allen, even though he had known her for only a short while at that point, could tell how shaken she was by the effect the stranger had had on her. Allen looped his arm through hers, and looked at her with a question in his eyes.

"Oh," Nicole said brightly, trying to keep him from guessing how flustered she was, "I just came out to take a walk around the garden. I love paper lanterns glowing against an evening summer sky."

"A poetic turn of phrase, luv," said Allen, taking her hand, "which is part of the reason you're already doing so well at the Pelican. Your descriptions of the art brings the light of possibility to a prospective patron's imagination."

"Oh, Allen," Nicole smiled, "you do love to exaggerate. And it's you who has the turn of phrase. Now, stop flattering me, and let's see how the guests out here on the patio are managing."

Allen turned to her and placed his warm hands on her bare shoulders. "They're managing much better, I'm sure," he said, "than I ever could without your help."

At that moment, Ren Steele stepped out through the French doors near the Koi pond. With him were an elderly lady dripping with diamond jewelry and a beautiful young woman in a turquoise outfit. Both seemed to be attending ever so closely to whatever remarks he was making. Nicole smiled briefly at the group, determined not to make a fool of herself again. She felt more sure of herself holding on to Allen's arm than she had since her dark eyes had first locked on to Ren Steele's light blue ones.

"Nicole," Allen said, "here's some ladies you should meet." He gaily motioned Ren and his two companions over to the palm tree they were standing beneath. "It's ever so perfect that we should all be here like this," Allen enthused to the group. Nicole stood mutely, barely listening, almost unable to breathe, as Allen made the introductions and carried on some spirited small talk about the gallery opening and local happenings. He was charming to the ladies and polite and respectful toward Ren. Nicole found herself wonder if she could ever learn to be comfortable on cue around so many different types of people.

"I'm sure my assistant Nicole would be happy to show you around," Allen was saying. Nicole was startled from her thoughts at the sound of her name and, not wanting to appear as if her mind had been drifting, was quick to agree. "Of course," she stammered.

"Then it's settled," said Ren Steele. "I'll be here around two o'clock tomorrow. Now, I'm afraid, we need to be going. Thank you so much for an interesting evening." His eyes bore into Nicole's with a glint of amusement, and he was gone.

"Oh, darn," said Nicole. "I'm sure he'll be insufferable to deal with."

"Why do you say that, my dear?" inquired Allen. "He seems fairly well-bred to me, considering that they say he spends most of his time out in the swamp."

Nicole blushed faintly and was thankful to be standing in the orange glow of a paper lantern. She hadn't been aware that she'd spoken her thoughts aloud. "Oh, I don't know. it's just a feeling I get that he's rather high-handed. Let's not waste the night talking about him, if you don't mind," she said, tugging Allen playfully inside to the makeshift dance floor. As she put her arms light around Allen's shoulders, she wondered briefly if Ren Steele was a good dancer.

The next morning, Nicole was little annoyed with herself when she noticed she was dressing with particular care. She had been resolved to proceed with the day as if there was nothing special on her agenda, just the usual showing of art to customers ant he scheduling of future exhibits. However, there seemed to be a little spring in her step and a song in her heart. She had put on a cream colored silk suit and stepped into bone calf heels. No, she thought, I'm not doing this. She changed into jeans, heels, and a business-y shirt and jacket.

She gave more thought to the necklace she had chosen. It was filigreed ivory. Her grandfather had brought it home from a business trip to Pakistan decades ago and had given it to her mother. She loved the craftsmanship and the way the ivory lay against her tan skin, but she took it off. Elephants had died for these essentially meaningless baubles. Maybe I will donate it to a charity auction, she thought.

Nicole felt a slow rise of sadness at the memory of her father. She had loved both her parents, but had been closer to her mother. He father had been a rather remote, complex man who showed his affection for Nicole through his deeds more than through his words. Their relationship had only started to warm up once Nicole was out on her own. She had felt they were getting closer in every way just over the past year, and to have lost him just as she was getting to truly know him was almost more than she could bear.

At 7:15, Nicole stepped out into her little walled courtyard entryway with a steaming mug of coffee, and picked up her newspaper. She took some time to breathe in the warm air and admire her little garden. The cheery morning sun was spilling over the wall onto the brick patio floor. Her large pots of colorful mixed annuals brightened the space. Ferns and vividly colored coleus grew in clumps in areas of deeper shade.

She sat at her patio table, and took a sip of coffee, which was just cool enough to drink. As she finished the coffee, she browsed through the paper, looking for news or advertising pertaining to the art world. Part of her job was to place announcements and paid advertising for the gallery, and she kept track of what competing operations were doing as far as their publicity.

Just before 8 am, Nicole locked the patio gate behind her and got into her car. As she drove along the palm-lined streets and boulevards, she admired the Spanish-style architecture of the home and businesses.

Naples used to be a quiet and sedate town; now, traffic could b a problem during the middle part of the day, when the many retied residents were out running errands and doing their shopping. Normally, what would be rush-hour traffic in most places wasn't so much of a problem in this retirement-oriented community, but in the mid-winter high season, a visit to the post office or bank could take quite a bit of time. There was a slow, relaxed feel to the area's business transactions that sometimes made Nicole impatient if she was in a hurry. Lines in banks could move quite slowly as customers' business activities were peppered with small talk with the tellers. Photos of family members and even of pets were bought out for comment as the people in line chatted with their favorite teller.

The head teller at the bank the Pelican Gallery used was a breezy, efficient young woman with long black hair, which she variously wore pulled back in a knotted pony tail, braided or beaded, or loose around her shoulders.

Each daily change of style evoked good-humored comment from the retired male customers. She seemed to take it all in stride as she processed the paper work and counted out bills with snappy, efficient style. Nicole rather enjoyed listening in on the banter most of the time.

At a doughnut shop, Nicole stopped to pick up a cup of coffee and six chocolate glazed doughnuts. The Pelican Gallery was just around the corner, but Nicole had discovered that she seldom had time during the morning to go out for a break.

By 8:30 am, Nicole was unlocking the double entry doors to the gallery. Millie, the bookkeeper-receptionist, wouldn't arrive until 9:00, so Nicole re-locked the doors, punched in the deactivation code for the alarm system, and crossed the shiny marble floor to her office.

One of the many things Nicole loved about working at he Pelican was the beautiful, spacious rooms. On her first day of work, when Millie had shown Nicole to her new office, she had wondered if there had been a mistake. Millie had said no, indeed, that Mr. Davies had specifically told her that Nicole would be occupying this particular space.

Today, as almost every day, Nicole stopped to admire the room as she crossed the threshold. The focal point of her office was clearly the dark gray sofa, done in fat, thirties-style upholstery. It was extremely comfortable, as clients usually remarked, but its styling was svelte as well as voluptuous. The floor-to-ceiling bay windows behind the sofa were covered with translucent ivory fabric screens framed in light oak. They provided filtered light and complete privacy. A long kilim rug woven in warm, subtle hues of deep peach, brown, and gray was laid parallel to the couch in the center of the room over a white tile floor. Nicole's desk was styled in clean, contemporary light oak and birch. Large, framed prints of some of the gallery's publicity posters were lit by track lighting. Nicole looked forward to the day when, perhaps, a poster announcing her own show might be hanging there a well.

Millie put through a call from Allen just after nine o'clock.

"Good morning, chickadee," Allen sang, "and how might you be today?"

"Very well, Mr. Davies," Nicole replied formally but with a smile in her voice. "And how may I be of help?"

"Nothing special right now," Allen replied. "I'm just calling to check in. I won't be coming in until late. I have a meeting at the bank, and then I have to make a quick trip up to Ft. Myers to look at some mixed media. Gloria Anton. Do you know her/"

"No," admitted Nicole. "What does she do?"

"Oh, abstracts with a kind of a shore-line-at-dawn feel to them. I'm going to take a look, to see if we might bring some in. What do you have today?'

"Not a lot. I'm finishing up the publicity plans for the shows next month, and I'm going to look at some advertising layouts for *Florida Sunset* magazine.

"Steele's still coming in today, isn't her?" Allen asked by way of a reminder.

"I suppose so," Nicole said cautiously, her heart beat suddenly thumping.

"He sounded as if he meant it, to me," Allen remarked. "Maybe you can sell him one of those Vilney lithos."

"I'm not sure what he's really interested in," Nicole replied faintly.

"Well, then, do the best you can with him. Ta-ta."

Nicole ended the call with a sigh. She hadn't entirely forgotten about en's appointment, but she had done her best to put it out of her mind. What in he world could she show him, she wondered?

Millie buzzed Nicole's intercom. "Mrs. Arbooth and Cindy are here."

Nicole rose from her desk and went to the reception area. A tall, thin woman of about seventy, wearing a pastel blue suit, was holding a miniature schnauzer. "We'd like to see some paintings to go over our sofa, wouldn't we?" Mrs. Arbooth said, directing herself to Cindy. "We are tired of beach scenes, bu we still like pictures of flowers, don't we?" She said, cuddling her dog. "Do you have anything we might like?" She asked, turning to Nicole.

"We have some lovely pastels of hibiscus blossoms," Nicole suggested, leading Mrs. Arbooth across the galley room to a display of florals mounted in gold-tone frames.

"Ooh," said Mrs. Arbooth, "look at those, Cindy. Do you have anything larger? Our sofa is rather long."

"How about something like this?" Nicole offered, showing a gilt-framed oil of pink and white water lilies floating in the foreground of a pool with a stand of lotus leaves and flowers behind them.

"That's nice," commented Mrs. Arbooth. She turned to a display wall on Nicole's left. "We were thinking more of something that goes better with yellow. Do you have any daffodils?"

"Not right now," Nicole admitted, "but I can show your a nice oil painting of some forsythias.'

"Ooh, Cindy," cooed Mrs. Arbooth, "let's get this one.'

Nicole smiled as she took down for Mrs. Arbooth the good-sized, impressionist-style oil of a vase of forsythia sitting on a glass table.

"Does the price include the frame?" Mrs. Arbooth inquired, as Nicole prepared to begin packaging the art.

"It sure does, and we even load it into your vehicle for you.'

"Can you come hang it for me, too?"

Nicole had been surprised the first time she'd gotten such a request, but she had quickly come to understand that positioning and hanging heavy framed pieces was not always something her customers could do for themselves.

"Not today, I'm afraid, but we could schedule you for later this week."

"Never mind, I'll just ask Elmer across the court. He'll do just about anything for a home-cooked meal," she winked.

Not long after Mrs. Arbooth and her dog had left, a tall, thin man came in and asked to see some bird lithographs. He selected without much comment a portrait of two Florida Brown Pelicans nested in some mangroves. The artist had produced almost photographic detail of the birds' feathers and pouched beaks in subdued, natural tones. The artist was a favorite of the area's many bird-lovers.

When she had finished with the pelican-man, Nicole returned to her office, and pulled out a sketch pad. She roughed in a quick line drawing of an oak tree thickly hung with Spanish moss, and began to contour and shade it. She was a little disappointed with herself for not having made more tie for her own artwork. But, she reminded herself, within the few weeks since she'd finished her art school courses, she had moved, furnished a new apartment, and was becoming oriented to a new job. "Don't expect everything so quickly," her mother had often admonished. Nicole nodded at the memory.

"OK, mom, I'll ease up just a little bit," Nicole said aloud to herself. She picked up her coffee, and let Millie know that she'd be outside for a bit.

Nicole exited through the French doors leading to the gallery's side patio and garden area. She went over to a stone bench positioned by a small fishpond and seated herself for a moment's relaxation.

The sunlight played on the pool's fountain, casting rainbows and sparkles on the surface of the water. In the quiet corners of the pond, out of reach of the falling droplets, six- to ten-inch long Koi nibbled greedily around the lily pads and submerged plants. The water was perfectly clear, but looked black because of the color of the pond liner. The golden-orange and pearl white fish were bright against it.

Nicole had heard that Koi could be trained to be hand-fed. She had brought out some of their food pellets to give it a try. She got up, stretched, and then knelt down by the side of the pool. She slapped the surface of the water with the palm of her hand to attract the fish, and offered a pellet held between her thumb and forefinger to a pearl which Koi with a bright orange blotch in front of its filmy, transparent dorsal fin.

"Come on, sweetie pie. Come take it, take it," she cooed.

"I'm game. What are you offering?"

Nicole looked up. She felt the color and heat of a deep blush rising in her face. Ren Steele stood tall above her, a wide grin on his face.

"Nothing," blurted Nicole, getting to her feet. "I mean, I was talking to the fish," she muttered. "I was feeding them."

Ren held his smile. He looked at his watch. "It's almost lunch tie, isn't it?'

"I thought you said two o'clock," Nicole replied, still feeling silly.

"Ah, you did remember." Ren held her gaze until Nicole dropped her eyes.

Why does this man make me say such idiotic things? Nicole chided herself. She straightened and smiled politely, as she would at any customer. I will not make a total fool of myself, she vowed.

"Mr. Steele. Welcome to the Pelican Gallery. Would you like to come see what we have on exhibit today?'

Ren's eyes briefly scanned Nicole. "I'm sure what you have is very nice," he said, following her in to the main part of the gallery.

"If you like water colors, Mr. Steele, you might appreciate these." Nicole indicated a matted arrangement of pastel-colored washes suggesting the early dawn color changes of a garden pond.

"Did you do these?" Ren asked.

"No, Mr. Steele, none of this is my work," Nicole replied pleasantly.

"How about these?" Ren asked, crossing the floor to a display of bright acrylic abstracts.

'No, I'm afraid not."

"Good," said Ren. "I've never had much interest in abstract art."

"What is it that you do like, Mr. Steele?" inquired Nicole.

Ren turned to her, and looked her over. "Well," he drawled, "I appreciate color and passion. But I like to be sure of what I'm looking at."

"But, that's just the point, I believe. The color and the passion."

"Are you up to giving me art appreciation lessons, Miss Carpenter? Because, if you are, I'd be very much interested in learning more. In fact, I don't thing there's anything I'd enjoy more today than to follow you around these rooms, listening to you," he said softly.

Nicole swallowed. She again felt the warmth rising in her cheeks.

Ren stepped closer to her. The expression on his face had softened. Nicole felt her eyelids grow heavier, and her full lips slackened a bit. Ren looked at her mouth, and smiled.

"Show me what you like best," he suggested quietly.

Nicole raised her eyes to his. "Are you toying with me, Mr. Steele?" she asked.

Ren didn't reply.

Nicole was aware of her heartbeat, and of the quiet in the room.

"Show me what you like," he repeated gently.

"Very well, Mr. Steele," Nicole said primly.

She stepped away from him, to a lithograph of the rear elevation of a glass and concrete house with tall expanses pf windows revealing the first and second story interiors. "I like this," she said.

Ren looked at the picture. "It's a little cold, I think. Although the fireplace warms it up. What do you admire about it?" he asked, turning once more to face her.

"I like how the clean, sharp lines of the house contrast with the lush, topical foliage of the landscaping," Nicole replied.

"Ah, you are giving me art appreciation lessons," Ren remarked with a smile.

"You asked Mr. Steele," she returned coolly.

"I did, at that. And now, I'd like to ask you something else."

Nicole's breathing slowed. What kind of a man was this, she wondered? Simple conversation with him left her feeling hot and thick and slow moving. He was getting the best of her without seeming to try. Was it entirely in her imagination that their conversation seemed to proceed on multiple levels? How was she to take hem? She thought of Ren with the blond woman at the reception last night.

Who was she to him? A girl friend? His fiancee, perhaps. Nicole straightened, refusing to fall under his spell.

"What's that, Mr. Steele?"

"Are you hungry?"

"Hungry?" asked Nicole, feeling disoriented once more.

"Yes. For lunch."

"Lunch?" Nicole stammered.

"You know. The meal people take around this time of day."

Nicole's flush deepened. Was this man trying to make a fool of her? If so, she was certainly doing a good job of appearing to be a complete idiot for him. In each of their two encounters, she had quickly been reduced to stammering and blushing like a schoolgirl. She couldn't bear to think of how she would behave if she had to have a whole meal with him. She would spill her iced tea, and drop pieces of salad in her lap. What did he want with her?

Ren continued to gaze at her.

"Why are you here, Mr. Steele?" Nicole asked a little desperately. "I don't think you came to see art."

"I do appreciate beauty," he said, looking into her eyes. "Especially natural beauty."

Nicole thought again of the svelte, expensively dressed woman with Ren at the gallery reception last night, and of how she had seemed to hang on to his every word. She tossed her head. "I'm sorry. I can't have lunch with you," she said curtly. "Some of us have to work for a living."

Ren's jaw tightened, and his eyes grew remote. "I'm sorry to have bothered you," he said coolly. Without another word, he turned and strode out of the Pelican Gallery.

After Ren had left, Nicole sat in her office, spinning the words of their encounter through her mind. Had she misjudged him? Had she offended a potential customer of the gallery, and perhaps even behaved unprofessionally? After all, her boss had introduced them at his party, and, although she couldn't remember exactly how it had been arranged that Ren would come to the Pelican, she did recall that a definite appointment had been made.

Nicole shook her head, remorseful and chagrined. She just couldn't seem to focus clearly when he was near her. She blushed and stammered and kept getting lost in his eyes in mid-conversation. Perhaps the way she had declined his invitation to lunch could been been taken as nothing short of rudeness. Just last week, an older gentleman had asked her to join him for an iced tea after he had looked at some small granite sculptures, and while Nicole had not accepted his invitation, she had taken care to be courteous and kind as she declined. It would never have even occurred to her to treat a patron or a prospective customer with anything other than a professional, sympathetic attitude. Nicole sat back in her chair, feeling mortified. She fervently hoped that nothing else would go wrong with her day, and that she could never again have to encounter Ren Steele.

Shortly after two pm, Millie buzzed Nicole's intercom, and announced that Marta Andress would like a word with her. Allen had told Nicole when she was being oriented to the business that Marta was a buyer for the gallery, but she had never met her and knew nothing else about her. "have her wait just a moment, Millie," Nicole requested. "I'll be right out."

Nicole was just rising to go greet this Ms. Andress when her office door was practically flung open by a woman of about thirty with long, gorgeous auburn hair, and an imperious flash of green eyes. She was model-slim, and was dressed in a royal purple suit with a short skirt. A Hermes scarf was tossed stylishly around her shoulders.

"I don't care for how the Lippincott etchings are hung," she announced by way of a greeting. "Have we had any interest in the Michaud abstracts, yet?" she asked, quickly taking in Nicole's office décor. "I see you've wasted no time settling in."

Nicole was at a loss to respond, not wanting to say the wrong thing, and not being entirely sure of the importance of this woman's relationship to the gallery and its business operations. "Where's Allen today?" Marta asked, seating herself on Nicole's office couch without waiting for Nicole to respond to her questions about the art.

"He said he was going to Ft. Myers to look at some paintings," Nicole replied politely. "Is there something I could help you with?"

"I doubt it," Marta said, getting up. "Just tell him to call me, and please do something about the Lippincotts."

With that, she sauntered out of Nicole's office, leaving behind a strong scent of Opium perfume.

A few days later, Nicole was at her desk finishing up some work, when Allen strolled in to her office. He leaned his shoulder casually against the door frame and smiled when Nicole looked up.

"How's it going?"

"OK, I guess," replied Nicole with a faint smile. "How's it going with you?"

"Not bad. But I'm getting a bit tired lately of racing around the Gulf Coast. I could use a change of pace, I think. What abut you? Would you like a change?"

"That might be nice," Nicole said noncommittally.

"Great!" enthused Allen. "Then, I have a scheme that would give us both what we want." He beamed at Nicole, who looked up at him questioningly.

From his pocket, Allen pulled a sheaf of airline tickets. "I need you to fly up to Orlando, and to fetch a package for me. You leave Monday at 10:15 in the morning, and your return flight is booked for 4:20pm the same day."

Nicole looked doubtful. She did not enjoy flying, and, in fact, had not been on an airplane since before her parents had died. She knew that, sooner or later, she would have to confront her fears, but Allen's request took her by surprise.

"Can't you just ship it air freight?" Nicole asked hopefully.

"I'm afraid not, ducks," Allen replied. "I need someone to pick it up from the warehouse, which is quite near the airport, just a short taxi trip; you can hire one at the airport."

"How about if I just drive up and get it for you?" Nicole asked, still hoping to avoid a plane trip.

"I'd really prefer it if you flew," replied Allen. 'It's a good two hundred miles one way, and your car isn't running like it should, am I right?"

"No, it isn't," Nicole admitted.

"I'll tell you what," said Allen with a twinkle. "You pop up to Orlando and pick up the package, all the while having a nice break from the routine around here, and I'll get some one to look after your car while you're gone. Deal?"

Nicole nodded. It was thoughtful of Allen to recognize that she might need a change of pace. It would be nice to get way from the Pelican for the day. She smiled. He was becoming like a friend to her, a dear friend on whom she could rely. "Tell us all about it, Ducks," he would say, coaxing Nicole out of a troubled mood. And Nicole did feel lighter when she shared her concerns. How she missed her regular telephone visits with her mother. She really needed to start making some new friends, now that she was settled in at the Pelican and at her cozy apartment.

****

Nicole tossed in her bed. The light of a half-moon filtered across her sheets. Her comforter lay flung on the carpet in a heap. It was still too early for the night air to have cooled enough for her to need even a cotton sheet, but Nicole knew, if she ever managed to fall asleep, she would get too chilled under the ceiling fan to sleep with no cover at all. Unfortunately, there seemed to be little chance that she wouldn't still be awake when the dawn light slanted through the white fabric-covered shutters at her bedroom windows.

She sighed, and stared up at the shadows playing across the textured plaster ceiling. The ceiling fan oscillated gently. A ray of moonlight was striking the small brass bead at the end of the chain in such a manner that it appeared to danced erratically above the center of the bed like a firefly.

After another hour of watching the glowing red numerals of her digital alarm clock change as the minutes passed, Nicole sat up and hugged her knees.

She swung her feet onto the plush carpet, silver in the filtered moonlight, and slipped into a soft robe. Her bare feet padded across the living room carpet and she stood near the window overlooking her courtyard garden. She couldn't sleep, but neither did she feel like turning on late-night television, nor flicking on a lamp and reading. Her head was buzzing dangerously close to a headache, and sharp light in her eyes wouldn't be helpful.

The moonlight, though, seemed inviting. Nicole opened her front door, and breathed in the cooler night air through the screen-paneled storm door. A fat moth rested on the screen, its shape in dark contrast to the faintly lit silver mesh. The night vibrated with the music of insects. Faint sounds of nighttime traffic drifted from a distance. Pulling her robe around her, Nicole stepped outside.

The patio bricks were still warm from the heat they'd absorbed during the sunny daytime. It was still too early and too warm for dew to have formed. Nicole stood in the center of the courtyard near her patio table and felt a small measure of enchantment beginning to crowd away some of her earlier humiliation.

The colors of the garden flowers were lost at night, save for the whites and yellows, which glowed softly as they lay against dark foliage. The scents of the night-blooming plants hung richly in the air. Nicole glided over to a patio chair, and sat down. Her thoughts were coming more slowly now, no longer racing, and her faint headache was receding. The tropical night, with its sensuous richness, was beginning to work its magic.

Nicole thought of her Aunt Jane, and wondered what she was doing now. Sleeping, probably. Or rocking on the Cypress Retreat's wrap-around, screened porch, listening to the night sounds of the Everglades.

Suddenly, Nicole wanted to be there too, rocking and talking, or maybe sleeping deeply, secure and safe, there with Aunt Jane, her mother's sister. In the wilderness, maybe she could collect herself, and perhaps begin to make some sense out of all the confusion and all the changes in her life.

She could walk, and paint, and listen to her Aunt's gossipy, entertaining conversation about the doings of the locals and the retreat's guests. Perhaps she would even find respite from the disturbing churn of emotion that she had not been entirely able to quell since she had first looked into Ren Steele's blue, blue eyes.

How could she ever satisfactorily explain to Allen her mad dash from the restaurant earlier in the evening? She would have to continue to go along with the charade—or rather, the lie—that she had become ill, at least until the incident had receded from Allen's mind, over a period of just a few days, if she were fortunate.

Perhaps, if she never saw Ren Steele again, the magic spell he seemed to have cast over her would dissolve and she would be able to forget that her knees had become weak and her body had trembled at his slightest, most casual touch. Perhaps she would eventually be able to forgive herself for the graceless way she had responded to his luncheon invitation. Perhaps, she would even be able to put back on track her hopes for a peaceful life in beautiful Naples, Florida.

As the sun began to color the western horizon, Nicole resolved to call her Aunt Jane to arrange a visit; she would come just as soon as she cleared, with Allen's permission, her schedule at the Pelican Gallery.

Nicole arrived late for work, just after nine o'clock. Allen was already in his office. He came out into the main room of the gallery when he heard Millie greet her.

"It's good you could come in today. I'd been a bit concerned that you might not have felt up to it," he said.

Nicole blushed slightly. "I'm sorry I created that bit of drama last night. I'm feeling perfectly fine today, and I'm sorry if you were worried."

"Was it a bit of a bug?" Allen asked.

"A bit of a..? You mean, a stomach flu?" Nicole hated to lie. "No, I'm fine today. I don't know exactly what came over me. I'm sorry you were so inconvenienced, having to take a cab home, and all."

"No problem whatsoever, Ducks." Allen smiled. "I'm just glad it was nothing serious."

Nicole hesitated. "Allen, I do have something I'd like to talk with you about."

Allen glanced at Marta, who had come in and seemed to be waiting for Allen to finish with Nicole. "Marta, do you mind? I'll just be a minute." Marta shrugged irritably, and sauntered off to her own office.

"What can I do for you?" Allen asked, ushering Nicole into his office and closing the door. He seated himself in his leather upholstered swivel desk chair, and motioned for Nicole to take a seat.

Nicole took a deep breathe. "Allen, you know how the other day, when I was telling you about my Aunt Jane, you offered me a little time off to go visit her? I was wondering if you meant it, and if so, is the offer still good?"

Allen studied her. "Has something come up?"

"No. I mean, yes." Nicole took another breath. "I was thinking last night after you took me home about her invitation to come for a visit, an I would really like to go. I know it's short notice..."

Allen waved his had dismissively. "Not a problem. Marta will be around quite a bit for the next several days.

She can manage any of your work that can't wait until you return. When would you leave?"

"Well, I was thinking of going tonight. It's really less than two hours away, I think."

Allen nodded. "I have your mobile number, but just leave me the telephone number there, in case I need to reach you."

Nicole smiled. The sun was shining brightly as she called the number for the Cypress Retreat.

Chapter 3

Traffic south of Naples on Highway 41 was thin, for a change. Many people heading east across the southern tip of Florida took Alligator Alley, by far the faster route. Even though Nicole had gone home to pack and to secure her apartment, she could still reasonably expect to reach the Cypress Retreat before full darkness settled.

Aunt Jane had seemed not the least bit put off by the short notice of Nicole's visit.

"Bring some Cutter's, if you have some," she reminded, referring to mosquito and insect repellent. "And some light-weight long pants, too, and good walking shoes that you wouldn't mind getting wet. I'll make sure I save some dinner for you. We're having my special southern catfish and black-eyed peas dish, but don't worry I fix it low-cal, low cholesterol. I'll save some for you. We really can't delay dinner around here—these birders get up early."

Once Nicole had passed the turn off to Everglades City, she set her car's trip meter to count off the miles. Only a painted wooden bird set on a post, the work of Fred, Jane's companion and business partner, marked the dirt and marl road leading to the Cypress Retreat. Nicole found the bird marker without difficulty, and turned onto the long private road.

Before Nicole had even finished parking, a fit-looking woman of about fifty emerged from a side of door of the lodge. Nicole got out her her car, and grinned.

"My goodness, girl, if you don't look the picture of your mother at that age! Come here and give your Aunt Jane a big hug!"

Nicole put her arms around her aunt's shoulders, and was enveloped in a warm embrace.

"I hate to sound like every other doting relative in the world," said Aunt Jane, "but you have grown up to be so beautiful! That hair—you must have been growing it long since you were about sixteen. I remember the high school graduation picture your mother sent me when I was still up in Alaska – it was just past your shoulders. Here, I'll have Fred carry in your bags."

"Fred!" she called. "Where is that man?"

"It's okay," said Nicole. "I can manage. They're not heavy at all."

"How were my directions? Asked Jane. "Good enough, I guess, or you wouldn't be here," she went on, not waiting for Nicole's answer.

"The part about setting my trip meter once I crossed Route 29 was a big help," replied Nicole. "I suppose you're used to giving directions out here."

"I sue am," agreed Aunt Jane. "There's something about these birders—maybe because they're so used to looking up in the trees—but about one in three misses the turn off entirely and ends up halfway to the Miccosukee Reservation before they figure out that something's wrong. Last weekend, Fred had to go out looking for a Canadian couple. Found them reading their map by the side of the road. Nice people, though. Spotted a Great Crested Flycatcher with a shed snakeskin in its beak while they were here. Nesting season, you know."

"Come on in, girl, you must be tired. Fred," Jane called again, "come meet Nicole."

A tan, vigorous-looking man in his late fifties emerged from the lodge. His overalls were spotted with mud, and his hands were black with grease of some type. "What in the world are you hollering about, now?" he asked. He spotted Nicole, and wiped his palms on his denims.

"Sorry for the way I look, Missy," he apologized, "but I was working on a boat engine." The way he emphasized his words suggested to Nicole that he was directing himself to Jane as an explanation for the delay in his greeting.

"Well, let's not just stand here," directed Aunt Jane, "or these bugs will eat us alive."

The Cypress Retreat was named both for its proximity to the Big Cypress National Preserve and for the type of insect-resistant wood from which it was built. The peaked roof of the great room rose to a height of perhaps twenty feet. A stone fireplace dominated the room. The slate floor was covered with slightly threadbare oriental carpets, on which rested large, comfortable couches and easy chairs arranged in conversation groups. On either side of the fireplace, tall bookcases set against the wall were filled with nature periodicals, wildlife reference books, and old issues of *National Geographic*. Card tables with stacks of board games and decks of playing cards were positioned near large windows. A couple of guests were reading beneath the warm light of floor lamps adorned with tasseled, ivory-colored shades.

"There's plenty to read around here," commented Aunt Jane as she led Nicole through the room, "which is a good thing, because we tend to cater to a pretty bookish clientele. There's some mystery novels, too, if you like them, and people leave some popular novels from time to time when they check out. "You probably like television, too," she said, looking back at Nicole. "We got satellite in not too long ago – Fred put up the dish himself. Cable doesn't come out here, of course."

"I'll take you to your room so you can get settled, and then we'll ear," she continued. "We eat family-style here," she said with a gesture indicating a dining room behind closed French doors. "I'm so glad you're here! Real family," she said with satisfaction.

Nicole's room was comfortable beyond her expectations. A queen bed of warm maple dominated the room. The walls were painted a light, warm ocher, and the floor was carpeted in a similar tone. There was a three-drawer chest beside her bed, and a dresser with a large mirror was placed against another wall by a tall window. A white china vase filled with pink flowers and green-gray eucalyptus stems was placed to one side of the mirror. The walls were hung with bird prints in subdued tones, and a small marble bust of Marjorie Stoneman Douglas had been positioned on the dresser opposite a vase of Coral Bean and Buttonbush.

"What a beautiful room," said Nicole as she began to unpack. "I never expected anything so nice."

"This is one of the nice rooms," admitted Aunt Jane. "Most of the others are just a little more rustic, like our brochure says."

"How did you decide to get this place?" asked Nicole.

"Simple," replied Jane. "I read about it in one of my bird magazines when we were still up in Alaska. "I'd gotten so sick of the cold by then, and especially those long dark winters—there's almost no daylight time up there at all in the winter, as I suppose you know—that I told Fred I was going to go someplace warm."

"He was pretty tired of the cold by the, too, so were put in an offer by telephone. Of course, we ad never actually seen this place at that point, other than the listing photos online, but your mother and father came down to look it over for me, so I felt pretty confident that it was what we wanted," Aunt Jane explained.

"I remember them telling me a little bit about your plans," said Nicole, "but I guess I was too wrapped up in school back then to have really given it much thought."

"Well, it's a lot of work," continued Aunt Jane, "but Fred's so handy, and we get some awfully nice guests. The thing about birders is that they don't seem to need a lot of entertainment, which is a good thing."

"Of course, some of them like to go to the Seminole bingo and so forth, that's not so far, and we arrange air boat tours of the Everglades. But, otherwise, it's quiet pursuits."

"Are you getting many artists?" asked Nicole.

"Some. I think I told you that we carry some art supplies in our little canteen. Watercolors, acrylics, that sort of thing. You could help me figure out how to get a better handle on what to stock, I imagine," she suggested, brightening at the idea.

"I'd love to," said Nicole. "I brought some of my own supplies along, in case I get a chance to do some painting."

"Hope you brought plenty of shades of green," Aunt Jane quipped.

Nicole, having finished unpacking, pulled on a blue and white striped long sleeved cotton tee shirt and a pair of khaki shorts. "What should I wear for shoes?" she asked her aunt.

"Well," said Jane, 'for tonight just those sandals should be fine. Tomorrow you'll need something to hike in."

"Are you happy here?" asked Nicole, putting away the last of her things.

"Yes, I seem to be," replied Jane. "Fred and I are used to each other. We get some interesting people in, and not too many difficult ones. Business is okay. The restaurant and bar are open to locals, so we get a few of those. More and more of them seem to be finding us, so some nights that bar can be a little lively. All in all, it's turning out to be what I hoped it would be."

Nicole smiled. "How long have you and Fred been partners? It seems like a long time, now. How did you two meet?"

"Actually," replied Jane, leading Nicole back down the hallway to the Retreat's common areas, "we met up in Alaska, not long after your Uncle Henry passed away. I had always been curious about the Iditarod dog sled race, and I went to see what all the excitement was about the first year I was up there. Fred was there, too, and I guess we just hit it off, both of use being what you could call outdoorsy types."

"Have you ever thought about getting married again?" asked Nicole.

"I don't know," said Aunt Jane, at something of a loss for words. "We get along together all right, and we're fond enough of each other, I suppose."

Fred, who was sitting at card table poring over some papers, looked up as Nicole and her aunt entered the room.

"What's that?" he asked.

"I was saying to Nicole that we're fond of each other, that's all," replied Jane. Nicole noticed that her aunt was blushing. "Let me get your dinner," she said, walking out to the kitchen though the French doors that separated that room from the great room.

Nicole sat down in a comfortable easy chair, and picked up a magazine.

"Are you all settled, Missy?" asked Fred.

"I sure am," she replied. "This place is so beautiful."

"It's comfortable," said Fred.

"Are you glad you moved down her?" Nicole inquired.

"Oh, yes. We were ready for a change, particularly your aunt. She's a trooper, but she was ready to leave all that cold weather."

"Are you from Alaska, originally?" asked Nicole.

"Montana," replied Fred. "Of course, when I was in the service, I got around quite a bit."

"Do you have children?" asked Nicole.

"A grown-up son. Up in Montana, still. I took care of him after his mother left us, but he's been on his own for some time now."

Nicole was silent, not wanting to pry.

"Your aunt's quite a woman," he went on. "Never met one finer."

"What's that?" asked Jane, who had returned from the kitchen.

Fred cleared his throat. "I was just getting a little it sentimental, that's all," he said,

rising. "Well, I guess I'll go out and get things ready for tomorrow."

"You do that," called Jane after his retreating figure, "and I'll get Nicole fed."

"What did you two find to talk about?" inquired Aunt Jane, leading Nicole into the

Cypress Retreat's large, homey kitchen. "Here, sit at the table, and I'll get your plate."

"Not much," said Nicole, seating herself. "We were just getting to know each other a little bit."

Jane put a steaming plate down in front of Nicole. "Cat fish and black-eyed peas,"

she announced, watching as Nicole tried a mouthful. "How is it?"

"Good," said Nicole. "Thank you."

"It's a dish I learned from some locals," said Jane. "I have to cook what they like, since, they're what keeps us in business during the summer months, mostly. We're the only restaurant around for miles," she smiled. "I'll have to get you to try some 'gator while you're here."

"Some…?"

"Yes, you heard right," grinned Aunt Jane. "Alligator. Tastes like chicken, just like you probably have read or heard. Only a little gamier. Don't worry, if you don't want to, my feelings won't be hurt. Most folks like it, if they don't know what it is they're eating. Some of the bird folks ask for it, after they've tried it."

"Well," said Nicole, taking a sip of coffee, "I'm not really too adventurous when it comes to food."

"That's okay," reassured her aunt. "More coffee? How about some pecan pie? I didn't make it, we get it delivered, but it's pretty good."

"No thank you," said Nicole. "I'm good for now."

"Well, then, let's put these dishes in the kitchen, and then we can go take care of the bar. We close early, but if you're tired, I can manage."

"No, I'm fine," said Nicole, getting up to help clear the dishes.

The Cypress Retreat's lounge was in a spacious area off the dining room, and it was dominated by a large, stone fireplace and three billiard tables. A flat screen television above the bar was tuned to a Marlins game.

"I can't wait until Fred puts up that satellite dish. The reception here is iffy," commented Jane. "Every one complains about it. We only get a few channels reliably. It'll really help business, I think, when we start getting all the sports channels. Do you like football or baseball?"

"I don't really follow it," replied Nicole.

"Well, then, it's good that it's not football season yet," said her aunt. "Here, it's the Dolphins, which everyone either loves or hates. Tampa Bay has really gotten popular, too, and with the satellite, we would get them, and the Jaguars, and probably all the rest of them. Of course, right now, it's the Marlins," she said, referring to the baseball game.

"Here, sit," said Aunt Jane, motioning Nicole toward a comfortable chair near a window. "What can I get you to drink?"

"Do you have any diet cola or diet ginger?"

"Both."

"A diet ginger, then," said Nicole, settling in to her large, overstuffed chair and stretching her legs.

Jane returned with their drinks and seated herself across from Nicole.

"Are you sure you got enough to eat?" she asked.

"Definitely. I'm stuffed. You're a good cook.'

"Well, I do like to learn, and to fool around in the kitchen."

"Do you cook all the meals, for all the guests?"

"I do quite a bit of it, but when we're the busiest, I have someone who comes in. Plus, I hardly ever do the lunches. I have Maria, who helps out a few hours a week. Makes the lunches for people who want 'em, and fixes something for anyone who isn't out exploring. Plus, she does some food shopping, and some prep cooking for dinners. I'm lucky to have her—she doesn't need too many hours—she has kids in school – and she works fast. Her husband brings in a lot of the fresh fish.

A grandfather's clock gonged at the half-hour. Nicole studied the clock. "is that clock the one grandma used to have?" she asked.

"The very same," replied her aunt. "I don't know exactly where she got it, but when she passed on, I got it, and I've had it ever since. That clock's been all the way to Alaska, and then, down here. Still keeps perfect time."

"What was grandma like when your were growing up?" asked Nicole. "i never really knew her—she died when I was five, I guess."

"Hard-working. Loved roses and gardening. And you know," she went on reflectively, "she had some artistic talents, too. She would sketch a lot in her spare time, and she did the most unusual needlework. Some of the pillowcases I've got here at the Retreat are her work. Your mother and I never really seemed to have any of the artistic talent, but, as you know, your mother was pretty much a fanatic about growing roses."

"What kinds of things did grandma like to draw?" asked Nicole.

"Well, when your mother and I were children, she would do all kinds of pictures—line drawings, really—for us to color with crayons. Fairy tale characters from the books she would read to us. They were so good that they could have been illustrations for a book. Of course, your mother and I weren't such good little colorers."

"Did you save any of them?"

"No, I'm sorry to say, but your mother might have. Did you see anything like that when your were closing up their house?"

"Not really," said Nicole. "I have lots of stuff that she saved for me—drawings I did as a kid, report cards, family photos, but I didn't see any drawings that grandma might have done."

Aunt Jane sighed, and closed her eyes. "That was the saddest day of my life," she said softly. "I never in my wildest dreams expected that I would get such a telephone call. Your mother and father were such a devoted, happy pair. You had made them so proud with how well you'd done at that art school. I still can't believer they're gone." She wiped her tears.

"I still can't believe it, either," said Nicole. "I miss them every day. I have been

feeling so disconnected from family, and from my roots."

"Well, now that we're in the same part of the world, more or less, we'll see more of each other, I hope." Jane took a sip of iced tea. "So...tell me more about your life in Naples. What's your job like? Have you got any social life, yet?"

"Well..." began Nicole, but just then Fred peeked in and cleared his throat.

"Sorry to interrupt, ladies," he began, looking toward Aunt Jane, "but could you please spare me a moment?"

"Of course," said Nicole, glad to have time to collect her thoughts. How to explain what seemed to have recently become her very confusing life?"

"I was wondering," continued Fred, "if you would be wanting me to get a hold of Quinn for an air boat ride, or a hike, tomorrow?"

"How's the weather supposed to be?" asked Jane.

"Same."

"Would you like to see some of the nature around here tomorrow? Quinn, and me, if I can get away, would show you some of our swamp life."

"Sounds great," said Nicole.

"Okay, then," said Jane, turning once more to Fred. "Ask him if about nine would work."

"I'm sure it would," replied Fred. "I'll get a hold of him," he said, turning to leave, "and you two have a nice evening, then."

"What a nice man," said Nicole, after Fred had left the room.

"That he is," responded Jane. "I'm lucky to have found him, that's for sure. It's not every man who would be willing to just pack up and come down here." She smiled. "But enough about us. How are you getting along in Naples?"

"Just fine," said Nicole. "I'm happy with my job, and I like my apartment."

"What, exactly, do you do at that gallery place—the Pelican?"

Nicole explained her duties at the gallery, described her apartment, and told her aunt a little about some of the customers and patrons.

"Sounds like it's just about perfect for you," commented Jane.

"Oh, it is," enthused Nicole. "I'm learning so much about the art business—the day-to-day operations, things you don't really learn much about in school."

"Do you see yourself sticking with it for a long time?'

"I really haven't thought too far ahead," replied Nicole. "It's perfect for now, at least. I would like to find more time to do some painting, but now that I'm pretty much settled in Naples, I'm sure that I'll be able to."

"I hope you'll come back out here to see us, now that you know where we are," said Jane.

"Definitely," replied Nicole.

"When?" asked Jane, with a smile.

"Well, maybe in a couple of weeks, if that isn't too soon."

"You know it isn't. You're welcome any time, the sooner the better. Oh, dear, there I go again with another one of my cliches."

Nicole suppressed a smile.

"Back to you," continued her aunt. "Are you seeing anyone special?"

Nicole's eyes darkened briefly. "No…" she exhaled. "We have quite a few social events in connection with the gallery, so I'm starting to meet people from around town. We had a reception at the gallery the other evening, and Allen's got a party coming right up that he said something about."

"Are you seeing Allen?" asked Aunt Jane.

Nicole hesitated, formulating her thoughts. "We do things together occasionally, but it's just casual, like friends. He's really taught me a lot about the business, and he's very warm and nice."

"Not a romance?" pressed her aunt with a smile.

"No, not as far as I'm concerned," said Nicole. "he's my boss, and he's a good, close friend."

Her aunt regarded her silently for a moment. "Have you met anyone else, yet?"

"No," said Nicole, and suddenly she thought of Ren. She felt a little warmth coming to her cheeks. She couldn't possibly begin to explain their confusing encounters, and besides, she didn't expect to see him again, not after the way she had behaved at the gallery.

"Naples is a pretty small town," Aunt Jane remarked, as if she were reading Nicole's thoughts.

"I suppose so," replied Nicole, "although it sure is busy in the winter months. You wouldn't believe the traffic. Nothing like Miami or Orlando, though."

"I don't think I'd care for it," replied Jane. "I've always preferred the great outdoors. Here, you wouldn't believe some of the creatures we have—some deer, raccoon, and squirrels, of course, and all the birds, insects and reptiles you could imagine. Tomorrow, you'll meet some of them when Quinn takes you out."

"I can't wait," said Nicole. "It's so relaxing here. Do you ever use that fire place?" she asked, getting up to inspect the stone hearth.

"All the time, believe it or not," her aunt replied. "Well, not much during the real heat of the summer, but more than you'd think the rest of the year. It doesn't throw off as much heat as you'd expect. Would you like a fire tonight?"

"I wouldn't want to trouble you..." began Nicole.

"No trouble at all. Fred," Aunt Jane called, "do we have any dry wood left?"

"What's that?" shouted Fred.

"Wood. Do we have any?"

"Sure," said Fred, coming in to the room. "I have a bunch of dead-fall stacked up out side the wood shed under a tarp. It's pretty dry. Why, does Nicole want a fire? Not worm enough for you?" His eyes twinkled. It was in the mid-seventies and humid.

"Of course it's warm enough," snapped Jane. "We just want to look at it for a while, while we talk, don't we?" she said, turning to Nicole.

"If it's not too much trouble," said Nicole.

"No trouble at all!" replied Fred.

In a minute, Fred returned with an armload of dry branches, and arranged them in the fireplace. "I'll throw these in, and I brought in a couple of logs that should bun for a little while," he said, lighting the kindling with a balled -up newspaper and a match.

Nicole sipped the mocha coffee her aunt ha served while Fred was preparing the fire. She stared at the flames as the kindling caught fire, and felt herself relaxing. The warmth felt surprisingly good against her bare legs.

"I could fall asleep here," she murmured.

"You've had a busy day. You just rest. I'm gong to see if anybody needs anything at the bar," her aunt said.

At the pool tables at the far end of the lounge, two men and a woman were drinking beer and playing a game of eight ball. Nicole couldn't quite make out their words, but she could hear the clicks as the balls struck each other and the low rumble as they were knocked into the pockets. The tone of the players' conversation was good-natured and was punctuated with quiet laughter.

Nicole's eyelids grew heavier as she listened to the sounds of the pool game, which now seemed very far away. Somewhere, a door opened, and greetings were exchanged. A man's voice, low and thick with the local accent, requested a draft beer.

"Get one for me, too, Lenny, would you?" asked a man whose voice was familiar, but so far away.

"Sure thing, Ren," Nicole dreamed. "Coming right up."

Nicole was asleep in her bed, in her room at her parents' home in Clearwater. Outside her open window, tree frogs chirped in the night. Her aunt was in the living room, and Fred, too, and they were talking about her.

She's just visiting for a little while, but she's promised she'll be coming back more often, her aunt was saying. Tomorrow, we're going to show her some scenes she could paint. I don't know quite what she wants to see. Wild orchids, Nicole dreamed, fragrant orchids. Hanging Spanish moss, mounds of lacy ferns. Cypress trees tall against the blue sky, their roots deeply embedded in the moist earth.

Nicole shifted in her chair, and her eyes were open now. The man sitting with her aunt at the bar, talking quite convivially, was Ren Steele.

He was dressed in jeans, boots, and a short-sleeved plaid cotton shirt that was open at the collar. A lock of his thick black heir curled over his forehead. His face and neck were tan. Nicole closed her eyes again. This wasn't possible. She was still dreaming. She was at her aunt's Cypress Retreat, at the edge of the Big Cypress swamp, and she was dreaming. When she opened her eyes and shook herself awake, Ren Steele would be gone.

But, from across the room, the talking continued.

"She drove out from Naples just this evening," her aunt was saying. "I hadn't seen her in years. I'd hated so to miss her mother's and father's funerals, but we'd just been down to Clearwater a few months earlier, thank goodness, so I didn't feel so bad that we couldn't get back down from Alaska so soon again. We'd had a wonderful, wonderful visit. I wanted to come, but we had just put down our savings on this place, and we were all tied up finishing up loose ends in Alaska. So really, I hadn't seen her since she was in high school."

Nicole opened her eyes, fully awake now. It was not her imagination. She wasn't dreaming. Ren Steele was seated at the bar, next to her aunt. His sharp, handsome profile was illuminated. His legs here draped casually around the bar stool, one booted foot resting on the brass rail.

Nicole inhaled quietly. Should she pretend to be asleep? Maybe he hadn't noticed her. No, that was ridiculous. Her aunt had been talking about her. It was inconceivable that he hadn't seen her as soon as he'd come in or while her aunt had been telling him about her visit. How long had they been talking? Maybe, if she got up very quietly, she could get to her room before anybody noticed her silent escape.

As soon as she'd thought the word 'escape', Nicole was seized with an almost overpowering desire to flee the room. Cautiously, she looked around; the hallway leading to her bedroom was about twenty feet from her chair. She would never make it. Her aunt would notice that she was awake, and she'd call out to her. It would be unspeakably rude not to respond, and then she would have to acknowledge Ren Steele's presence in the room.

Nicole exhaled quietly. She would just get up, face the introductions, and then it would be over. She rose quietly from her easy chair. Her legs felt unsteady, and her heart was beating madly. Her mouth had gone dry. How would she ever be able to speak? Maybe she wouldn't have to say anything. She could nod politely, and then leave.

"Oh, good she's awake," her aunt said enthusiastically when she saw that Nicole was standing. "Come here for a minute, honey. Here's some people I want you to meet."

Nicole nodded mutely, and moved toward the bar. It seemed to take forever to cross the room. She could feel

Ren's eyes on her, but she looked only at her aunt, at the wall behind the bar, at the man with Ren Steele, anywhere but at Ren himself.

"Nicole," her aunt was saying, "I'd like you to meet Ren and Lenny. They come in here once in a while, and I've been telling them all about your visit."

"How do you do?" Nicole murmured, amazed that she could get the words out.

"Pleased to meet you," said Lenny.

"A pleasure," nodded Ren, with a wicked smile.

"I was telling them what a joy it is to me that you have moved down to Naples, and how we plan to see more of each other from now on," said Aunt Jane, appearing oblivious to Nicole's discomfort. "Here, have a seat," she said, indicating an empty stool next to her.

Nicole was speechless. She felt like an awkward schoolgirl. Not knowing what else to do, she moved over to the bar stool and put her hands on the curved wood of the bar. If she sat down, she would be committing herself to stay put for a while. If she left, it would be rude.

"How long will you be staying?' asked Ren, with a mischievous glint in his eyes. It was as if he could read her indecision.

"Not long," Nicole stammered, surprised that her vocal cords worked at all.

"A couple of days," explained her aunt. "Tomorrow, I was saying you'll be going out with Quinn to take a look around. "Did I tell you she paints?" asked Jane, turning to the men.

Ren grinned. Nicole recalled him asking her, during his visit to the Pelican Gallery, which of the paintings on display were hers. He's enjoying this, Nicole realized with a flush. The moment had grown from awkward to intolerable. In her anger, Nicole found some strength. She would not be made a fool.

"Excuse me," she said, as politely as she could, for her aunt's sake. "I'm very tired, and I want to get up early tomorrow. It was nice meeting you," she said to Lenny, and with a venomous look at Ren, she fled from the room.

Chapter 4

Somehow, Nicole made it own the long hallway to her room, and flopped down on the bed. She buried her face in the pillow, her heart racing. How was it possible, of all the places in Florida, that she had run in to Ren Steele at what she had hoped would be the sanctuary of her aunt's isolated retreat in the Everglades? What on earth was the man doing out here in the wilderness? How had he come to be on familiar terms with her aunt? He had looked very comfortable and relaxed, as if this was not necessarily his first visit to the Cypress Retreat.

Nicole considered the contrasting worlds in in which she had encountered Ren. First there had been Allen's gallery party, where Ren had been formally dressed, and escorting, it seemed, two ladies. Her impression of him had been that he was just another handsome and, possibly, wealthy man, out for an evening party. Then, he had toyed with her at the gallery the next day. Why had he even bothered to come, she wondered? He had seemed more interested in distracting her from her work than in looking at art. How embarrassing, the way she had insensitively refused his luncheon invitation, but there had been no way she would have willingly spent her lunch hour with a man who was a difficult as Ren Steel. And, next—Nicole winced at the recollection of how she'd practically run out of the restaurant when she' d been with Allen. And now—to have to face him here, of all place, was simply unbearable.

How could she be expected t relax and continue to enjoy what she had so hoped would be a warm family reunion if she had to live with the threat of Ren Steele turning up to destroy her equanimity?

How well did Aunt Jane know this insufferably arrogant man? Nicole turned over, and stared up at the ceiling. Had they been talking about er as she slept? Nicole hoped her aunt hadn't told him much, but Aunt Jane did like to talk. She hated to think that he might know things about her life, when, to her, he was so…. mysterious was the word, she supposed. What was he doing out here? The Cypress Retreat was well off the beaten path. Despite herself, Nicole smiled. Her aunt's use of cliches might be catching.

Nicole sat up, and hugged herself, rocking a little bit. What she would do, if she were any other place else in the world, would be to pack up and leave immediately. Nicole envisioned herself driving back across Highway 41 to Naples in the dark, and retreating to the sanctuary of her quiet little apartment. But this she could not do. It would be impossible to think only of herself, leaving her aunt disappointed. Any explanation she tried to envision would be insufficient and, probably, not accepted by Aunt Jane, anyway. As much as she wanted to avoid Ren Steel, she would have to stay, and pretend to enjoy the remainder of the visit. Nicole dreaded the thought that she might have to see him again. How in the world would she manage? Suddenly, Nicole felt tears flowing down her cheeks.

Just then, there was a knock at the bedroom door. Nicole raised her had, and wiped here eyes. "Yes?" she answered.

"It's me, dear," called Aunt Jane. "May I come in?"

Nicole sat up straight, and checked her reflection in the dresser mirror. She smoothed her hair back behind her shoulders, and took a deep breath. "Of course," she answered. "The door's not locked. Come in."

Aunt Jane entered the room, and looked Nicole over. "I hope I'm not intruding," she began.

Nicole managed a smile. "No, you're not. Please, would you like to sit down?" she asked, patting the bed beside her.

Jane seated herself near the end of the bed, and leaned back against the curved foot board. "Do you like your room?" she began, a little hesitantly Nicole though.

"Of course. It's beautiful," replied Nicole. Then, it was her turn to hesitate. What should she say? She looked at her aunt and dropped her eyes. How to begin?

"How are you feeling?" asked Aunt Jane.

"Oh," replied Nicole, still searching for words. "I'm okay. A little tired."

"You left kind of quickly, I noticed."

Nicole smiled, despite herself. Her aunt certainly didn't miss a beat. "Yes, I suppose I did. I guess I just got so tired suddenly."

"Yes, I noticed you had fallen asleep out there for a while. Did we bother you, with our talking?"

Nicole looked directly into Aunt Jane's eyes. They were serious, without a trace of her trademark twinkle.

"I had been dreaming," began Nicole again. "I was dreaming that I was at mom and dad's house in Clearwater. I thought I was back in my old room, and when I woke up..."

"You wee upset that it was just a dream?" finished Aunt Jane. "You poor dear. It must be so hard on you." She sighed heavily. "I miss them, too, especially your mother, of course. What a horrible, horrible tragedy.'

Nicole dropped her eyes again. Would it be so wrong to let her aunt believe that she had reacted out of grief, stimulated by a sad dream? But, her dream hadn't been sad, and it ha barely been a dream. She had heard them talking…..

Nicole drew another deep breath. "Yes," she said slowly. "I miss them. But it wasn't really a sad dream. It was just….kind of confusing. I sort of heard you talking, in the background, and it kind of got blended in to my dream."

Now, it was Aunt Jane's turn to hesitate. "I *was* talking about you, Nicole. I was telling some friends a little about you. Maybe you heard that."

"Some friends?" Nicole asked.

"Yes, Ren and Lenny, those folks I introduced you to when you woke up."

Nicole was silent. Aunt Jane had called them 'friends'. That seemed to answer her question about how well her aunt knew Ren. Well enough, apparently.

"Does that trouble you?" she asked.

Did it trouble her that Aunt Jane knew Ren? Yes, very much, but it also piqued her curiosity. "Well..." Nicole hesitated. He aunt was her only family. She should be honest. But, how to explain?

"I'm just tired, I guess, and confused," Nicole replied. "I'm sure I'll be just fine in the morning."

Aunt Jane regarded her for a moment. "Well, then."

Nicole looked down. She was in the process of missing an opportunity to build closeness with her aunt by sharing her feelings. Her aunt seemed to know Ren. Perhaps she could tell Nicole what type of man her was, and shed some light on her confusion.

But, no. Now was not the time. She *was* tired. It could wait until later.

"Aunt Jane, I am so glad that I'm here with you, and that now we have the chance to get to know each other better. I've missed having family almost more than I can put in to words. I don't want you tho think, for a minute, that I don't want for us to be close. I'm looking forward to the next couple of days, and to all our future times together. I want to be very close to you. We'll talk abut a lot of things."

"We sure will," agreed her aunt. "And I'm really looking forward to your reactions to this part of thew world. I know you've been more of a city girl, but, as an artist, I think you'll find some real beauty around here."

"I know I will," agreed Nicole.

"Well, then," said Aunt Jane, getting up. "I'll let you get your sleep, and we'll continue our adventure tomorrow." She winked, leaned over and gave Nicole a quick hug, and left the room, shutting the door quietly behind her.

Nicole sighed, and got out of bed. She desperately needed sleep, but how could she hope to quiet her racing thoughts? She certainly wouldn't be very good company tomorrow if she didn't get some rest. Nicole crossed over to her window, and opened it wide. The humid night air was beginning to cool slightly. Nicole switched off the lamp by her bed, undressed in the dark, and put on the white, gauzy cotton nightgown she'd packed.

She got back into bed, and closed her eyes. At once, she began to wonder where Ren was. Had he left the Cypress Retreat, yet? Or, could he possibly be still out in the lounge? Did he have a place to stay nearby? When would she run in to him again?

Nicole turned over, and then sat up. What was it about the man that so unsettled her? She was quite good, she was finding from her work at the gallery, at talking with all kinds of people. Yet, with Ren, she could never seem to maintain any sense of self-control or poise for very long. Somehow, she would have to find a way to better-manage herself around him, should she encounter him again. She was uncomfortable at the idea of him being out here in the Everglades. It made no sense to her that such a sophisticated man was also apparently somehow a part of the quiet, rustic life so different from the art world of the coast.

Aunt Jane had said nothing negative about Ren, and, as forthright as she was, it was unlikely that she would spare an opinion or an observation. Nicole considered this. Of course, they hadn't actually discussed him. Nicole had been far too uncomfortable to ask any questions. She sighed. Perhaps if she talked with Aunt Jane about Ren, she would learn enough to allow her to behave more rationally around him if the future—if she ever saw him again.

Nicole settled back against her pillows, and pulled the sheet and light cotton blanket up to her shoulders. She closed her eyes. She was no longer feeling tired, but she hoped she would manage to get at least some sleep. There were no sounds coming from inside the Cypress Retreat, but outside her window, frogs were croaking. Nicole listened to the sounds of the swampland at night, and her breathing slowed. A night bird of some type was calling from far away. The hum of an insect chorus blended with the rhythmic song of the frogs. Or were they toads? Nicole wondered sleepily. She would make a point of finding out tomorrow.

In the morning, Nicole was awakened by a sharp tap at her door. "Rise and shine," called Aunt Jane. "Breakfast is served!"

Today, they would be hiking, Nicole remembered. She quickly dressed, putting on jeans, a coral short-sleeved tee shirt, and black high-top sneakers.

Nicole joined Aunt Jane at the kitchen table. "Am I dressed right?" she asked. Aunt Jane looked her over.

"i think you did just fine," she responded. "Put some Cutter's on any exposed skin, and tie back your hair, and we'll be on our way. We don't want to wait too much longer, because the bugs tend to get peskier as the day wears on. Although, fortunately, they are not yet at their seasonal worst."

"Are any of the bird-watchers coming with us?" asked Nicole.

"Oh, no," responded her aunt, "they went out at dawn. A couple are already back. It's almost nine o'clock. We'll be going out with a friend of mine, however, who I'm sure, you'll find colorful. His name is Quinn. He was born around here I'd guess about seventy years ago, and he knows every acre of this land like the back of his hand. We're supposed to meet him just up the path."

Nicole and Jane set out, taking a dirt path through the trees behind the Cypress Retreat. After a short distance, Nicole spied an old man sitting on a felled tree trunk. He wore a wide-brimmed camouflage hat, dungarees, and a brown shirt. His face was tan and well-lined. His brown eyes crinkled with his smile.

"Howdy," he said, extending his hand to Nicole. "All ready for our little walk? I hear you want to learn more about these parts. Quinn's the name."

Nicole extended her hand, and was surprised at the strength and vigor of his grip. "Pleased to meet you," she said. "I'm Nicole, Jane's niece."

"So I've heard," he replied, tipping his hat. "Well," he asked, looking at Aunt Jane, "are we ready?"

"Yes, I think we are," she replied.

With that, he turned up the path into the woods.

After about a mile's walk on the narrow pathway, the earth began to feel a little spongier under Nicole's feet. To the right, tall cypress trees grew in shallow, standing water. White wading birds with long, curved beaks and yellow legs stood watchfully as they approached. Garlands of gray-green Spanish moss hung from some of the trees, their strands as long as ten or more feet. Sunlight filtered to the forest floor, illuminating patches of ferns and leafy plants that looked like split leaf philodendrons to Nicole. The hum of insects rose as the three of them stopped in an open glade.

"Let's take a break here," said Quinn, "and I'll begin your education." He motioned for Nicole and Aunt Jane to sit on a fallen tree trunk.

Quinn tipped up the rim of his camouflage hat, and looked up.

"We are in the Florida Everglades," he began. "Is it what you imagined?" He was still looking up. Nicole looked up too, but couldn't figure out what Quinn was focused on.

"I'm not sure. I guess, if any thing, I thought it would be...swampier."

"You mean, wetter?" Quin asked. "Well, it has been dry this year, and we are in the tail-end of the dry season, anyway. But right now, we've been walking on what's known as a hammock, which is, more or less, semi-dry land. Actually," he continued, "the hammocks are somewhat like islands. The Everglades is made up of lots of these low islands, where, as you might have noticed if you know your trees, we have lots of pines, live oaks, cypress, palmetto, and so forth. There's also stretches of open water, actually grassy water, which is what the Indians named it –Pa-hayokee, they called it. Now, this grass," he smiled, "isn't what you'd find on a putting green. It's saw grass, which can get ten or fifteen feet tall. It's called "saw grass" because the stalks of grass are rimmed with tiny little teeth that are sharp enough to draw blood if you were to grab a handful and pull against the grain, so to speak."

"Now, the Seminole Indians made their way through this saw grass in dugout canoes. They lived in thatched chikees on the hammocks, and planted gardens, and hunted. And they fished in the open water."

"How could they stand the insects?" asked Nicole. Mosquitoes drifted about in the morning air, hanging close, but apparently sufficiently repelled for he time being by the Cutter's.

"Good question," replied Quinn. "What they did—and what some of us still do—was to grease their skin. Now," he continued, "life went on pretty much undisturbed through the first half of the 1900s, even as the rest of Florida went through its periods of boom and bust growth."

"Tell her about the flood control district," suggested Aunt Jane.

"Ah, well," muttered Quinn. "The flood control district. What can I say about it? Using polite language, I assume you mean," he grinned at Aunt Jane. "It's a mighty complex subject, and there's some awfully strong feelings that some of us have about it."

"It—meaning the Central and South Florida Flood Control District—was established back in the 1940's in an attempt to control the water flow that runs from Lake Okeechobee in a wide swath through the southern tip of the state, through the Everglades. And then out into Florida Bay. They built levees and dikes and canals that increased the water storage capacity of Lake Okeechobee, and that created thousands of acres of more or less dry land, which was, and still is, to a great extent, used to grow sugar cane, vegetables, and to raise cattle.

"Why is that bad?" asked Nicole.

"Depends on your perspective. It wasn't bad, necessarily, for the farmers who came, and it wasn't bad for what some of us call Big Sugar around here, meaning the cane-growing corporate types. And it wasn't necessarily bad for the locals who raised the cattle, and so forth."

"But, it's been bad for the Everglades ecology, and the wildlife, and for Florida Bay, south of here," interjected Aunt Jane.

"Basically," nodded Quinn, "their big drainage project increased the land area and decreased what was available for water-dependent animals and plants. Plus, in drought years, like back before you were born, in the early 1970's, the drought problem gets severely aggravated. When we get a fire, like that one we just put out a short while ago, the dried-out muck burns like a peat bog. And in high water years, the irony is, all their ditches and canals aren't really adequate to deal with all the water." Quinn sighed. "It's complicated. There's a lot of conflicting interests, let's just say. I hope, which is all I can do, that there continues to be awareness of just how important it is to try to re stabilize the Everglades and Florida Bay."

Nicole was thoughtful. "What about all the animals?"

Quinn looked at Aunt Jane. "There's a lot of people who care about he Everglades, and not just folks around here. All over the country, there's people and organizations who try to help save the Florida panthers, for example. Your aunt helps, in her own way, by educating her bird-watchers, and sometimes, grassroots efforts can do a lot of good."

"Are we likely to see any panthers?" asked Nicole.

"Not if they see you first," said Quinn. "There's not too many left, and they tend to stay out of the way of people."

"What do they look like?" asked Nicole.

"Like big, tawny cats, with golden eyes and long tails," replied Quinn. "I see them, once in a while. Just the other morning, I came across one sprawled out on a fallen tree trunk, snoozing in the sun."

"And alligators?"

"Those we have plenty of," he grinned. "But don't worry, they hardly ever get bigger than fourteen feet."

Nicole's eyes widened, and so did Quinn's smile. "They mostly eat turtles, little crayfish, birds if they can catch them. Occasionally, they do get someone's dog or pig, But they're mostly not aggressive, except for during mating season, when you would not want to bother them."

"Would we be likely to see any?"

"We could, indeed," replied Jane. "If we go out in a canoe into more open water, we almost certainly would."

"Is it safe?" asked Nicole.

"As long as you give them their space, and don't tempt them with your picnic," smiled Quinn.

The trio continued their walk at a more leisurely pace. Quinn led them in a wide circle, and Aunt Jane pointed out several species of birds for Nicole to identify using the bird book she'd brought along. It was close to noon when they arrived back at the Retreat.

"Staying for lunch?" Aunt Jane asked Quinn. "You know you're always welcome."

"Thanks, but not today," replied Quinn. "I've got to make a quick run down to Everglades City, but I'll be back this afternoon to take whoever wants to go on an air boat ride." he winked at Nicole.

"What's an air boat, anyway?" asked Nicole. She, Aunt Jane and Fred were seated in the Cypress Retreat's dining room, enjoying a light lunch of gazpacho, fresh bread, and broiled chicken Cajun-style.

"Well," replied Fred, "They're kind of a cross between a boat and a giant fan."

"Do they actually fly?" asked Nicole. Jane and Fred laughed.

"Not exactly. They stay on top the water. You'll see," said Jane. "It'll be easier to explain when you're there looking at one. But don't feel silly for asking. The bird people, at least the new ones, ask the same question all the time."

"Now," said Jane, pushing her chair back from the table and addressing herself to Nicole, "if you feel up to it, we have time to look at our canteen. I want to get your thoughts on artist supplies."

Aunt Jane walked Nicole over to a bright little room just off the main foyer of the Cypress Retreat.

"As you can see," said Jane, "we don't have too much in, yet. Most of the artists who come bring their own supplies, but they do ask for things."

"Like what, mostly?"

"Well, they name various colors of oil paints and acrylics. I try to get in the ones they ask for most – titanium white, mars black, and all the greens and umbers, and so forth."

Nicole looked at the tubes of color and the jars of mediums. "Well," she said, "you do stock nice brands. But, I would suggest that you keep plenty of Hooker's green and raw umber around at all times. Plus, you know those flat foam brushes with the angled edges like you can get at the hardware store? Some of those. Small ones. And some more angled brushed in all the sizes.'

Aunt Jane jotted some notes.

"You have a good selection of pre-stretched canvas," Nicole noted.

"You know what some of them ask about?" asked Jane. "Easels. But, in my suppliers' catalogs, they're so expensive. I don't know how many I'd sell."

"How about getting just a few light weight, quality ones, and renting them out by the day?" suggested Nicole.

"That could work," nodded Jane.

"What vendor do you use?" asked Nicole.

"Vendor? I just have these catalogs," Jane said, showing Nicole.

"Nicole glanced at the price lists. "I'm sure I could get your some better prices through the gallery on what I think you might need. I'll ask Allen when I talk to him."

"That would be nice," nodded Jane. "and, speaking of him, there was a telephone message from a Mr. Davies. Would that be Allen?"

"Yes, when did he call?"

"While we were out this morning. Apparently, he'll call back later. Fred took the message," she said, handing Nicole the slip of paper with the message. Nicole noted the time of the call from the Pelican Gallery's landline.

"Well, okay, I'll wait until he calls back," said Nicole.

"All right, then, you can get going down to where the air boats are," said Aunt Jane. "Fred will take you."

After a short jeep ride east on Highway 41, Fred turned off onto a hard-packed two lane dirt road.

"This is the old Tamiami canal," Fred announced. "What's left of it pretty much parallels the highway east and west across the state. We'll park here," he indicated. "The dock is just up ahead. We keep the Lodge's boats here."

Quinn was waiting at the dock for them.

"Well, Missy, here's your air boat. What do you think?"

Nicole regarded the flat-bottomed boat with what looked like a huge fan in a wire cage mounted at the stern.

"It looks like it could fly," she said, reaching out to take Quinn's extended hand as she stepped in to the boat.

"It'll sound like it, too," said Fred as he stepped into the boat behind her.

"You two take that seat up front," directed Quinn.

He fired up the engine, tossed the two mooring lines on to the dock, and slowly piloted the boat around so that it began to head into the main part of the canal. When they were clear of the docking area, Quinn throttled up the engine, and they began to skim over the water. He put the boat up on a plane, and Nicole was surprised at how smooth the ride over the calm, flat surface of the water was. Wading birds hesitated briefly at their approach, and then spread their wide, white wings, tucking their legs under them as they rose in flight and banked off away from the canal.

Nicole looked over the rail into the water, She was wearing polarized sun glasses, and although the water appeared to be almost black, she could see through to the bottom. Fish scattered and darted, arcing away from the boat. She could see aquatic plants growing almost o the surface in long tendrils of green.

"The water's so clear," she called to Quinn over the whine of the engine.

"Yup," he shouted. "It only looks black because of the color of the muck on the bottom."

Later, back at the dock, Nicole enthused, "that was so much fun. Almost like flying."

"It's fun," agreed Fred. "Almost like flying, or at least almost as loud."

"The tourists like it." put in Quinn. "But, its not the best way to see the wetlands."

"Why is that?" asked Nicole. "It seems like we traveled pretty far pretty quickly."

"Scares everything," retorted Quinn. "You noticed how the birds took off? Hiking or canoeing, you can move in quietly without so much disturbance."

"I think you'd like canoeing," agreed Fred. "Jane loves it. She considers the air boats to be a nuisance. Some of the visitors like them, though, and like you said, you can cover a lot of distance in them."

Later that evening, after a southern dinner of barbecued chicken, greens, sweet potatoes, and pecan pie, which they ate in the Cypress Retreat's dining room with the lodge's guests, Nicole joined some people for a game of darts in the lounge. Fred had lit a fire in the stone hearth, and the big room was cheerful with the conviviality of locals and guests. Nicole felt comfortable and chatty as she joined in the fun of the game.

"So, when is the rainy season going to start?" asked one of the lodge's visitors.

"A couple of the locals snorted. "Who knows? It's still a little early. We can't count on it until June, or so."

"Is the dryness due to El Ninõ?" asked the visitor.

"Maybe. They're blaming everything else on it," laughed another.

"I heard something about some fires not long ago," volunteered Nicole. "I was flying in a small commuter plane, and when we were beginning to descend into Naples, I was told that the smoke and haze was due to fires in the Everglades."

"Yup, we had some fires. They're all out for now. Not to worry."

"Who put them out?" asked the visitor. "It hasn't rained much yet, you were saying."

"Well," laughed one of the locals. "It wasn't the Miami fire department."

"You guys did it yourselves?'

"Us. Rangers. Volunteers. It's all we can count on, a lot of the time."

Nicole listened as the dart game continued. She thought about what Quinn had said during their morning walk about how the water flow through the Everglades had been altered when farming and development took off in South Florida.

"What kinds of people volunteer?" pressed the visitor. "Isn't it dangerous?"

"There's certain techniques to fighting outdoor fires. We get the job done. As to what kind of people—well, ones who care, and ones whose livelihoods or lifestyles depend on the Everglades."

"For example?" pressed the visitor. "I'm here on a personal vacation," she explained, "but I work for the *Miami Herald* in the features department. I'm not exactly doing research, but it's gotten to be a habit of mine to ask a lot of questions when I go someplace. I get ideas for stories that way."

The locals exchanged a look, Nicole observed, as soon as the woman said she worked for a newspaper.

"Well," drawled one of the men in his best swamp accent, "we do have our share of local color and small-town heroes, but I'm not sure that *Miami Herald*-type exposure is what we're really looking for out here."

"That's about right," seconded another. "Couldn't your just image," he snorted, turning to his pal, "how cute it would be if there was a picture in the Sunday features section of Ren Steele cradling that fawn in his arms, his face all sooty?"

"He'd kill us," said the first "and I wouldn't blame him a bit."

"Where could I find him?" inquired the woman, now suddenly in reporter mode, pulling out a notebook.

"Who knows?" evaded the man who had said the name 'Ren Steele'", as he wandered off to the bar.

Nicole turned away thoughtfully. Ren's name had come up again, and now she learned that he fought fires and had, in a sense, the protection of these local people. The man was as mysterious as he was complex, apparently.

Aunt Jane approached Nicole. You have a telephone call, dear. It's that Mr. Davies. You can take it in my office, if you like."

"Hullo, Nicole?" Allen said brightly when she picked up the landline. "How are you making out?"

"Just fine, Allen. How are things at the Pelican?"

"Not as good as they'd be if you were here. How's life in the land of mosquitoes?"

"Well, I'm not going to say there aren't any, but we have our ways of coping with them."

"We?" he inquired. "Are you becoming a swamp-woman already?"

"Not exactly," joked Nicole, "but you'll know when it happens by the pungent smell."

"Well, you sound happy. Are you having a good visit?"

"Wonderful. You should meet my aunt. She's terrific."

"I'd like to." He paused. "Do you think it would be all right if I drove out tomorrow? Maybe I could spend the night, if it's okay with your aunt, and we could drive back to Naples together. I could bring somebody to take your car back."

"I'll ask Aunt Jane just to be sure, but I believe it would be fine. When would you be arriving?'

In the afternoon, I guess. I have some work to do first at the Gallery."

"If I gave you a list, could you bring out some art supplies with you? Aunt Jane's going to sell them to the artists who come here."

"Sure, what should I bring?" Allen asked. "I'll write it down right now."

Nicole described the colors and the types of brushes and told Allen about the idea of renting light-weight easels to the people who needed them.

"Sounds great.," Allen said, "I'll see what I can bring along. Sleep well."

After she got off the telephone, Nicole found Aunt Jane working behind the bar.

"How was your telephone call?" Jane asked. Nicole picked up a clean dish towel and began to dry the mugs and glasses that her aunt had washed.

"Oh fine," said Nicole. "Allen would like your permission to drive out here tomorrow afternoon. He's going to bring some art supplies."

"That's nice" said Aunt Jane mildly. "Would he be spending the night? We have a couple of available rooms, as far as I know."

"Possibly," said Nicole. "He said he'd like to."

"It would be interesting to meet him. Do you think he'd like to go out on an air boat, or anything like that?"

"I'm not sure he's really the type," said Nicole. "I wouldn't plan anything."

"Well, then, we'll just leave it that he's coming, and we'll play it by ear."

Nicole smiled and gave her aunt a hug. "I guess I'll take a shower and think about getting ready for bed if we're through in here."

"We are for now. The place doesn't close for a little while, and we get some late people occasionally, but you go ahead."

"All right, I'll go clean myself up, then."

"Okay, you do that."

After a warm, relaxing shower, Nicole massaged a floral-scented moisturizer into her skin. She put on a long white cotton nightgown and sandals. She opened her bedroom window, and inhaled the humid night air. Around the corner from Nicole's room, at the end of the wing, was a cement slab patio with two benches, each flanked with barrels planted with cascading pink and white petunias. The night air seemed tempting.

Nicole slipped into her soft, yellow robe, and opened her bedroom door. The hallway was quiet. The door leading to the patio was just a few feet away. Nicole padded down the hall and opened the screen door quietly.

She sat down on one of the benches. A half-moon was rising, and lit up the puffy, towering clouds of the tropical night. To the east, the clouds were darker, and Nicole caught glimpses of heat lightning flashing far away. Maybe the dry season would be over.

Nicole heard a rustle near the shrubbery behind the bench, and stood up. Maybe it was a deer, or a raccoon. She looked around quietly, and then inhaled sharply. The tall figure of a man was outlined with silver from the light of the moon. He stepped quietly onto the patio, and Nicole gasped.

"What are you doing out here?" Nicole hissed,

"I might ask the same of you," said Ren Steele.

Nicole clutched her robe around here. "I didn't know you were here tonight."

"I stopped by a little while ago. I was just leaving now."

"What are you doing back here?"

"I'm parked just over there," he said, indicating where with the jerk of his thumb. "I saw you sitting on the bench."

"I didn't; know you were here," Nicole repeated, feeling foolish as she heard herself saying the words again.

"I'm glad I came," Ren said quietly, stepping closer. "You're quiet a vision n the moonlight."

Nicole stood her ground. "You frightening me. I thought your were in animal in the bushed.'

Ren grinned. "Maybe I am."

"What do you want?' Nicole demanded.

"Well, since you asked..." Ren said softly, and then his arms were around Nicole, and he was kissing her. Nicole, in her shock and surprise, was limp in his arms. His breath was warm. His mouth dropped to her neck, and she could feel his lips moving on her bare shoulder as he murmured something Nicole couldn't make out. Nicole shivered with the sensations of his warm lips on her bare skin. She closed her eyes, and her body seemed to mold itself against his lean, muscled torso. He groaned, and brought his lips to her mouth again. Nicole grew dizzy as the kiss went on and on. Her arms found their way around his neck, and she pulled away from his kiss, her eyes half-closed.

"I have to go inside, now," she said raggedly, turning away from him.

"See you tomorrow," he whispered after her.

No, not if I see you first, she thought, closing the patio door.

Chapter 5

Nicole opened her eyes and stared up at the ceiling fan slowly oscillating above the bed. She had been dreaming, bu the dream had faded already, and she couldn't remember it. Something important had changed. Her slender body felt heavy and lethargic. She felt as if even her blood was flowing thickly through her veins.

With the slow motions of a swimmer, she sat up. Her long hair lay thick and damp down her neck and back. She lifted it away with her hands, and let it fall back behind her shoulders. Her lips felt puffy and a little bruised.

Nicole dressed slowly and then brushed hes hair and put it up in a high pony-tail. She looked at herself in the dresser mirror, and touched her mouth. She thought of Ren's kisses, and dropped her eyes from her reflection as she felt color rise in her cheeks and her lips grow warmer.

When she had finished dressing, Nicole found a note from her aunt pinned up on the bulletin board in the kitchen near the telephone. Aunt Jane had gone out, and wouldn't return until later in the morning. Coffee was made and food was set out.

After drinking a cup of black coffee and eating a poached egg and a slice of cheese on an English muffin, Nicole packed a bottle of water and an apple into her back pack, along with a few tubes of acrylics, small jars of matte and gel medium, and some drawing pencils. She selected a light easel stand and a rectangular pre-stretched canvas from the Cypress Retreat's canteen.

Still felling a little like a sleep walker, Nicole set out on foot up the trail through the woods that she and Quinn and Aunt Jane had taken the morning before. Sunlight filtered through the high tree tops, and illuminated patches of dark green vegetation with light, golden yellow.

Nicole set up her easel stand in a small clearing, still moving slowly and dreamily. Keeping her mind clear of thoughts that were hanging in the background, waiting implacably for Nicole's later attention and consideration, she looked with her artist's eyes at the surroundings. She observed the shapes and natural composition, and noticed where patches of sunlight cast bright illumination, and how the shadows deepened the greens of the foliage and the browns of thick tree trunks. Patches of Spanish moss were caught in the branches like wads and tendrils of furry, gray-green yarn.

Nicole sketched out with a quick, sure hand the compositional elements of the woodland scene. She opened her tubes of color and squeezed out dabs around her palette. With her favorite angled brush, she stoked the color onto the canvas.

The morning sun rose higher, changing the play of light and shadow of the scene. Nicole painted rapidly, and a moody, impressionistic tropical glade sprang on to the canvas. At the focal point was a glistening pool of dark water. The figure of a woman knelt at the edge of the pool with long gleaming hair hanging down, concealing her face, the lines echoed in the Spanish moss spilling from the branches of sheltering trees. Nicole darkened the mix of the colors, and the scene was transformed from day to night, the glittering light on the dark water from an apparent moon.

The painting finished, Nicole absently cleaned her brushes and repacked them in her backpack. She organized the rest of her supplies. The canvas was still wet.

Nicole sat down on a tree trunk. Insects buzzed around the glade, and Nicole hoped that none would settle on the drying paint. She wiped a strand of hair from her face. The day was heating up rapidly. She twisted open her bottle of water, and took a long drink. Sh e was aware of a slight headache, and putting on her sunglasses, she began to massage her temples.

She allowed herself, for the first time, to think about the night before, and Ren's kisses. She touched her face near her mouth again, remembering the sensation of Ren's warm lips. She closed her eyes. The night seemed like a dream, now. In the hot, humid afternoon, it was hard to imagine what had come over her last night.

Now, as the insects buzzed around her, and birds called from the trees, Nicole tried to review the events of the night before, searching for clues to make sense of it. Why had Ren come so late to the Cypress Retreat? What had she done, or said, that would have given him license to kiss her? Nicole felt hot anger begin to rise in her throat. The man had some nerve. He had startled her. He had taken her by surprise, and had used the advantage of her shock.

Only some form of emotional paralysis would explain her own behavior, though. Otherwise, she would certainly have pushed him away immediately when he had taken her in his arms. Instead, Nicole had lifted her own arms around his neck and had held on almost desperately as he had kissed her into a dizzy turmoil. She had not slapped him, as he surely had deserved. Instead, she had simply wandered back to her room like a woman who was walking in a dream.

No wonder men like Ren Steele got away with their insufferable behavior, Nicole thought angrily. Well, it wouldn't happen again, Nicole vowed. But, of course, she supposed, good manners and conventional behavior were too much to expect out of someone like Ren Steele.

Nicole glanced at her watch. Allen would be coming soon she realized. Quickly, she gathered up her art supplies, putting the collapsed easel over her shoulder, and carrying the wet painting carefully. She make her way back across the hammock, and, arriving at the Cypress Retreat, she saw Allen's sports car parked by the side of the lodge. Suddenly, Nicole felt ill at ease. Her two worlds were colliding, she thought, and then wondered at herself for having such an idea.

****

Allen Davies had draped himself comfortably around a wooden chair and was watching Aunt Jane prepare lunch. He was wearing a pair of comfortable, expensive-looking pants, leather deck shoes, and on open-necked pink shirt. His wavy, dark blond hair was combed back from his face, except for some locks that curled over his tanned forehead.

He looked up when her heard Nicole enter the room, and a broad smile sprang across his face.

"You found us alright, I see," Nicole said brightly. "Have any trouble?'

"I missed the driveway entrance—by a few short miles," Allen joked, "but thanks be for cell phones."

"When he called," said Aunt Jane, "he was only at the Monroe Station. Not too bad for a first try."

"I might have missed it coming from the other direction if it hadn't been for your man waiting at the drive way," said Allen.

"Fred came out to look for him," Aunt Jane explained to Nicole.

"What have you been up to?" Allen asked Nicole. "You look...warm."

"I expect it's the heat," Aunt Jane answered evenly for Nicole.

"I went out into the woods to paint," smiled Nicole.

"Oh, let's take a look," said Allen.

Nicole held up her painting. Allen studied it, as did Aunt Jane.

"Your perspective came out well enough, and the figure's placed nicely in the scene," Allen commented.

"What's she doing?" asked Aunt Jane, referring to the woman in the painting.

"It has sort of a reference to Narcissus from the Greek myth, doesn't it?" Allen noted.

"I hadn't thought of it that way at all," Nicole said slowly.

"That's a good girl," Allen laughed, "letting your subconscious supply the archetypes."

"What's he talking about?" asked Aunt Jane.

"It reminds him of a story from Greek mythology," Nicole explained, "about a man who falls in love with his own reflection."

"Is that what they teach you in art school?" asked Aunt Jane, setting four bowls of salad on the kitchen table.

Fred came in from out back, and extended his hand to Allen. "Didn't get a chance to say much to you out at the road. Pleased to meet you."

"How do you do," Allen said, shaking his hand. "Allen Davies here."

"Welcome to the Cypress Retreat."

"Thank you very much," replied Allen. "It's quite a place you have here. When Nicole was telling me about your operation, I had envisioned something a little more primitive."

"Well, compared to some of the resorts you have in Naples, I'm sure it is," interjected Aunt Jane.

"We like it, though," added Fred.

"Have you had a chance to look around?' asked Nicole. "I'm sorry I was late getting back. I lost track of time, I guess."

"Well, that's what holidays are all about, aren't they?" said Allen brightly. "A chance to get away from all the burdens of civilization, especially the clocks."

"Speaking of which," said Fred, "is lunch ready? I'm so hungry I could eat a bear!"

"I'm sorry?" exclaimed Allen, seating himself at the table next to Nicole.

"It means he's hungry," said Aunt Jane. "What do they call it in England?"

"Lots of things, some of them utterly incomprehensible to Americans, I'm sure," replied Allen, "but I have never heard mention of a bear in that context."

"Chalk it up to a little local color, then," said Fred, digging in to his plate of chicken and yellow rice.

"This is great," said Allen, spooning a heaping pile of steaming rice onto his plate. Sort of Cuban, but not so spicy."

"That's right," said Aunt Jane. "A lot of the guests are retired, and they don't seem to care so much for hot, spicy dishes."

"How is the business going?" inquired Allen.

"Oh, it's a little slow right now. We have a Canadian group here, from the Toronto area. Actually, we've been getting quite a few Canadians."

"Really," responded Allen.

"Yes, they seem to like Florida as a vacation destination, as I suppose you know, and some of them find their way to us."

"They do, eh?"

"You sound like one yourself, with that 'eh'," remarked Fred, serving himself another helping of the chicken and rice. "Is there anymore iced tea?" he asked Jane, who had gotten up to take care of some of the guests eating in the dining room.

"In the refrigerator," she called.

"Here, I'll get it," said Nicole, going to the refrigerator.

"Well, I have spent some time in Ontario," said Allen.

"That would explain it," said Fred.

"Maybe you know some of the guests from there that we've had recently," said Aunt Jane, carrying over a tray of pies.

"I wouldn't think so," said Allen.

"It's a pretty small world, nowadays," commented Fred.

"A lot of the bird people like wildlife artists, such as...oh, Nicole, who's that artist that does bird paintings that I like?" asked Aunt Jane.

"You like Robin Sloan, you said," answered Nicole, pouring some more iced tea for herself and Allen.

"Yes, the same one your mother used to like. Do you know Dr. and Mrs. Albert Smythe, from Hamilton?"

"Sorry, doesn't sound familiar," said Allen

"How about Gerard McCloskey? Wasn't he from one of the universities in Toronto?" Aunt Jane asked Fred.

"I think so," he said, munching on a bread stick.

"Sorry, no," said Allen.

Nicole noticed that Allen seemed uncomfortable. He was answering Jane and Fred's questions politely enough, but he looked as if he wasn't enjoying their efforts to determine if they knew anyone in common.

"How did you find your way to Naples?" asked Aunt Jane. "Nicole said you were English."

"I emigrated to Ontario, and then just followed the line of cars south on I-75," joked Allen.

"Had you studied art in England?" asked Aunt Jane.

"Yes, I had gone to an art school in Liverpool, and then, I studied economics in London."

"Do you have family?" Aunt Jane asked, returning to her inquiry. Nicole smiled down at her hands in her lap. She knew that behind her aunt's get-to-know-you line of questioning that she was trying, in her own way, to be protective of Nicole.

"I have a sister," said Allen, and my parents are back in London. They're getting on, now, and have been giving thought to retiring, as you call it here."

"That's nice," said Aunt Jane.

"May I help you clear the dishes?" Allen asked getting up.

"Sit, sit," directed Jane. "We still have pie a la mode for dessert. Who wants what? We have pecan or apple, with vanilla or peach ice cream."

"Just a small slice of apple for me, please," said Nicole. "No ice cream."

"You, Fred?"

"The works," he replied. "Two scoops of vanilla on a big piece of pecan."

"Allen?"

"I'll have the same as Nicole."

Nicole followed Aunt Jane into the kitchen to help with the desserts.

"Thank you for lunch," said Nicole. "You work so hard."

"Sure, it's work," said Jane, "but I'm doing what I've always wanted. I don't mean the food part of the operation so much as the general hospitality end of it. I truly enjoy all the interesting people we get in."

She paused. "You know," she said, turning to Nicole,"there's something familiar about Allen."

"What's that?" asked Nicole.

"I don't know, exactly. I'll have to think about it."

"Do you mean you've met him before?"

"No, nothing like that. I don't think I've ever laid eyes on him."

"What, then?"

"I'm not really sure," said Aunt Jane, more to herself than to Nicole, handing Nicole a tray of desserts. "Like I said, I'll have to think about it."

Nicole carried the tray back to the table where Fred and Allen were waiting. Fred was talking about fishing.

"I did some great fishing when we were up in Alaska. You wouldn't believe the size of some of the salmon. Do you ever go out fishing in the Gulf?"

"Haven't yet, sorry," said Allen, tasting his apple pie.

"Well, you really should. A day on the water is like nothing else. Myself, I've been meaning to get down to the Keys to try some bone fishing."

The Keys aren't a bad drive from here, are they?" asked Nicole.

"I'd say about four hours to get down in to them," replied Fred.

"What are bone fish?" asked Allen. "Any good to eat?"

"Not really," said Fred. The name suggests what they're like. People fish for them on the flats, for sport. They put up quite a fight. Nowadays, you'd release them."

"Seems a little pointless, then, doesn't it?" remarked Allen.

"Like I said, its done for sport," replied Fred evenly.

"Well, sure," Allen said agreeably, "People do all sorts of things for sport, don't they?"

"Stranger things than bone fishing," nodded Fred.

"How was the pie?" asked Aunt Jane, returning from the kitchen.

"Great," said Nicole. Allen and Fred nodded their assent, mouths full.

"Nicole, why don't you show Allen around?" asked Aunt Jane. "I have a few guests coming, and I want to be sure that everything is ready for them."

"Would you like a tour?" asked Nicole, turning to Allen.

"Indeed, I would," replied Allen brightly. He stood, and thanking Aunt Jane and Fred warmly for the meal, he took Nicole lightly by the elbow. "Where should we begin?"

"Have you seen the great room?" Nicole asked.

"Yes, very homey," replied Allen.

"I just love the fireplace."

"Do they actually light it?" asked Allen, regarding the large stone hearth.

"Yes, but mostly for atmosphere in the evenings," replied Nicole.

"I suppose that's what most fireplaces are used for now, aren't they? Atmosphere, I should think."

"What do you think of the bar and lounge area?" asked Nicole, indicating the space with a gesture.

"Very rustic," nodded Allen.

"Have you seen the guest rooms?"

"Just mine, when I put my luggage away. Quite nice."

"I just love the way mine's decorated," said Nicole. "It's way down at the end of a corridor."

"So's mine," said Allen. "Do you suppose it's the same corridor?"

There are two wings," said Nicole. "Mine's off the main dining room."

"Mine's the other wing, I think," said Allen. "Too bad," he said with a grin. "I'm sure your aunt planned that."

"Probably," aid Nicole. "She's protective."

"Understandable," remarked Allen. "Perhaps if we were engaged, or something, she'd be less protective."

Nicole looked up at Allen. His eyes were crinkled with his smile.

"Would you like to walk around and see the grounds?" invited Nicole.

"I suppose," said Allen. Are there any snakes?"

"Possibly. This is the Everglades."

"Should I wear my rubbers?"

"Pardon?"

"Galoshes. Boots, to you," smiled Allen.

"Oh, one of your English terms. No, that won't be necessary. All of the Everglades is not swamp, you know. We're on dry land. Throughout the area are hammocks, which are dry, like islands in the swamp."

"I see you've been learning about the surroundings," said Allen, following Nicole out though a screened door.

"I have," agreed Nicole. "I've been walking quite a bit, and we took an air boat ride yesterday. It's really quite beautiful here."

"If you say so," Allen said, rather doubtfully.

"Yesterday, Aunt Jane and I took a walk with one of her friends. It's so peaceful and wild, I guess is the word."

"You haven't missed us, then, while you've been trekking through the swamp?"

"Well," smiled Nicole, "It's only been a couple of days."

"Some of the customers at the Pelican were asking after you."

"Really?' asked Nicole. "Which ones?"

"Ronald Scott came in. He said he'd been hoping you'd give him some ideas for his foyer."

"Did he decide on anything?"

"Marta showed him some etchings. He said he'd consider it further. He asked when you were coming back."

"What did you tell him?"

"I didn't know quite what to say, so I said you had taken a short holiday to visit your aunt."

"Oh," said Nicole noncommittally.

"Do you like it here?"

"I do," replied Nicole. "It's relaxing and, of course, its been so good to see Aunt Jane. She works so hard, but she seems happy with her life here."

"It seems a hard way to earn a living," remarked Allen. "She can't have that much business out here, can she?"

"She appears to do well with her marketing. She is building a following, apparently, and she does have guests coming and going."

"There doesn't seem to be much to do around here, does there?"

"Well, there isn't too much in the way of nightlife, if that's what you mean."

"No," agreed Allen, "it's hardly Miami Beach."

"I think the people who decide to come here consider that to be in its favor."

Allen laughed. "I suppose it takes all kinds. Myself, I prefer civilization."

"If you consider Miami Beach to be civilized," retorted Nicole.

"Nightlife and all the beach activity can be fun, don't you think?"

"Why did you decide on Naples for the gallery, then?" asked Nicole.

Allen Shrugged. "i like the Gulf Coast well enough. The Pelican is well-situated for our type of customer."

"Had you thought of the Miami area?"

"I had. Marta had looked at some properties there, and had made some initial inquiries. But, in the end, we decided on Naples."

"Any regrets?"

Allen looked warmly at Nicole. "None at all."

Nicole smiled up at him.

"What is it that you find so attractive out here?" Allen pursued. "Anything other than your Aunt's friendly and gracious hospitality?"

"Being with Aunt Jane is most of it," Nicole agreed. "She's not much like my mother, really. They look a little bit alike, or course, but Aunt Jane is so much more outdoorsy and outspoken than Mother was. Mother could also get along well with most people, and she did love her flower gardens. But she was more the tea rose and garden party type. It was hard for her to understand why Aunt Jane preferred to live what mother called her "frontier life"...Montana, Alaska. She would have certainly considered the Cypress Retreat to be set in a type of frontier."

"I'd have to agree with her," Allen said, looking up at a towering stand of cypress trees growing a distance away on a hammock. "It's hard to believe that people make a living out here. I don't mean those few, like your aunt, who manage to make some type of a business thrive. I mean, the local people. Where do they work?"

"This isn't a thickly populated area," said Nicole.

"No, I should think not," grinned Allen.

"Most of them live a basic, simple life," said Nicole.

"You've met some of them, I take it? Besides your aunt's lodgers?"

"A few local people come in, mainly in the evening," explained Nicole. This was a topic to stay away from, she thought to herself.

"Really," commented Allen. "What are they—hunters, fishermen?"

"Most people who live simply out here do some of that. I don't really know what all they do to get along out here," she said thinking of Ren.

"Most of them are probably on the dole," remarked Allen.

Nicole looked at him blankly.

"Government assistance," Allen clarified.

"I don't know," Nicole said. "Florida isn't exactly known as a welfare state.

"Well, we'll leave this serious topic to those who do. Let's talk about something more exciting."

"Such as?" inquired Nicole.

"Such as," said Allen with a smile, "you and me. The future."

Nicole looked up at Allen with a serious expression. You mean the gallery?"

"That would be some of it," he said. "The gallery. I could use a good partner."

Nicole glanced at him quickly. "I thought you and Marta were partners."

"We are," Allen nodded. "I meant more in terms of a long-range, full partnership."

Nicole said nothing. She was watching a hawk circle overhead. It drifted lazily on the air currents. She wondered what it was seeing from its vantage point, high above the trees.

"Are you with me, Nicole?"

"I'm not exactly catching your point," Nicole said, still following the hawk with her eyes.

The hawk swooped gracefully, and with a shrill cry, snatched a smaller bird in its talons. A few feathers drifted earthward as the hawk soared away, clutching its prey.

"How sad," said Nicole.

"Survival of the fittest," shrugged Allen.

Nicole looked at him. It was as if the incident had not affected him.

"That bird could be a mother," said Nicole, chidingly.

"So could the hawk," returned Allen.

Nicole studied his clean-shaven, handsome face. His blue eyes were clear and untroubled.

"You're right," Nicole said slowly. "But it's a shame that some creatures must die so that others may live."

"That does seem to be nature's way, though, doesn't it?" Allen said a little irritably. "The fish and meat on our table..."

"I know, I know," sighed Nicole.

"You're a sensitive artist," said Allen, draping an arm casually around Nicole's shoulders. "I shouldn't wonder that you would find that bit just then unappealing." He looked around the hammock, and then down at Nicole. "If I may speak frankly," he went on, "I'm not sure what the appeal is for you here. With your talents, and your style, I think of you as being much more at home in fine surroundings, with beautiful things."

"I'm comfortable here," Nicole said. "But, you're right, I like beautiful things."

"I'd love to surround you with beautiful things," Allen said softly.

"But you have, Allen," Nicole replied lightly. "At the Pelican, I'm surrounded with beautiful things. I have a beautiful office space. The little garden pool is one of my favorite places to sit and think. The art we bring in to the gallery, some of it I love."

Allen was silent. Nicole looked up at him carefully. It was as if he had more to say, but was holding back his words.

"Nicole," he said finally, "we really do need to talk. I'm not sure if this is a proper time..."

"Would you like to sit down?" she invited, indicating a fallen tee trunk.

Allen seemed to be looking at something on the tree trunk. "I don't think here's the spot," he said. Nicole looked more carefully at the tree lying across the tall grass and underbrush. It was swarming with insects.

"Oh, look," she said. "I'll have to ask Quinn about these," she said, inspecting the insects.

You do that," said Allen. "Me, I'll take a nice deck chair."

"To each his own," Nicole replied lightly.

"I wouldn't have you any other way," Allen said with a smile. "You're perfect as you are."

"I didn't know we were talking about me. I thought we were discussing vacation preferences."

"Then, speaking of such, how do you regard cruises? For example, for one's honeymoon?"

"That's a question out of left field isn't it?" replied Nicole quizzically.

Allen seemed uncomfortably at a loss for words. Nicole looked at him with some surprise. He'd always, until the present moment, seemed to her to be fluid and at ease with small talk or business talk.

"Are you ready to go back?" she asked finally.

Allen sighed. "Yes, I think that would be best."

They made their way back across the hammock in silence. The air was still and humid. Cumulus clouds towered overhead.

"Maybe it will rain soon," Nicole said. "We could use some. The fires," she said, looking at Allen.

"Yes, I'd read in the papers," he replied. His brow was damp with perspiration. "Any around here?"

"There has been. I'd heard they're out, or at least under control."

When they were in sight of the Cypress Retreat, Allen breathed an audible sigh of relief. "A nice, cool bath and some tea would be nice," he said.

"I'm sure you can be accommodated," Nicole said with a little smile. Her expression changed. Ren Steele was walking toward them, apparently coming from the Cypress. His face was grim.

"Look who's here," exclaimed Allen. "He doesn't look to be in too pleasant a mood," he said, looking back at Nicole. She had stopped in her tracks.

"No," she muttered. How had Ren managed to pick this moment to reappear, she wondered with annoyance. Allen was right, Nicole decided, he definitely looked...serious. She would do her best to keep her composure, no matter what degree of provocation he instigated.

Nicole took a deep breath as Ren drew nearer, and straightened to her full height.

"Good afternoon," she said pleasantly.

Ren seemed caught off guard. "Good afternoon," he muttered.

"Ren, you remember Allen Davies, one of the owners of the gallery where I work in Naples. Allen, as you surely recall, this is Ren Steele." Nicole was pleased at herself for having civilly conducted the introductions.

"Mr. Steele. Nice to see you again." Allen extended his hand. Ren looked at it, and then clasped it with his own in a brief handshake.

Nicole felt a gurgle of laughter rise in her throat. Here they were in the middle of the Everglades, and she was introducing the two men in her life as if they were in a drawing room. Nicole couldn't entirely suppress her giggle, and then felt a familiar flush of embarrassment. After her brief moment of composure, she was once again reduced to school-girl behaviors. And where had that thought come from—the two men in her life? She was dating neither one of them and nor did she have any desires in that direction.

"So, Mr. Steele," Allen said politely, "do you spend much time around here?"

"Sometimes," Ren replied curtly.

"Is that so?" Allen said.

"Yes, that's so, Ren said flatly, glaring at Nicole.

"You've run in to Nicole, then, I take it."

Ren looked at him briefly. "I'm acquainted with her aunt."

"How nice," said Allen. He turned to Nicole. "Are you ready to get back?"

"Give me a minute, please," Nicole said, hearing her voice say the words and wondering where they were coming from.

"As you wish, my dear," said Allen with a nod. "I'll see you back at the lodge, then." He turned to go with a slight furrow creasing his brow. Nicole and Ren both watched him in silence as he walked away.

"So," Ren said, "what's he doing out here?"

"Well," Nicole hesitated. "He wanted to drive out here."

"Why?" demanded Ren. "Are you two seeing each other?"

"And how would that be any of your business?" Nicole replied archly.

"I would hate to think of you with a guy like that," Ren said with a slight sneer.

Nicole's temper flared. "It's completely out of line for you to criticize a polite, civilized man who has never been anything but...polite to you," Nicole finished lamely.

"Is that the best your can come up with?" asked Ren derisively. "That sounds pretty lukewarm to me." He sounded satisfied.

"I think I've had enough of your boorish, presumptuous rudeness," said Nicole, turning to go.

"Is that so?" Ren said, reaching out and taking Nicole's arm.

He pulled her around to face him. Nicole regarded him coolly, taking note of the icy fire in his blue eyes.

"What is your problem?" she said finally.

Ren said nothing, staring into her eyes, still holding on tightly to her forearm.

"Please let go. You're hurting me."

Ren released his grasp, and Nicole turned to go.

"Nicole..." Ren said.

"What now?" she asked impatiently.

He laid a hand on her shoulder, more gently, and turned her slowly back so that she was facing him. Nicole felt a flush begin to spread across her face and chest. Her legs felt weak. Ren was staring at her mouth. Her lips parted under his gaze. He slid the hand on her shoulder slowly and gently behind her head and spread his fingers up through her hair. Nicole shivered with the sensation as he curled his fingers slightly, lightly raking her scalp and then pulling her head back a degree.

Nicole helplessly noted the blaze brightening his eyes even as they darkened as his pupils dilated. She closed her eyes with a sigh, and felt his breath warm on her cheek. His mouth covered hers in a deep, warm kiss that clouded her senses and disoriented her.

Fearful of falling backwards, she grasped his broad shoulders, and felt his hard muscles beneath her fingers. A dizzying need to surrender to him was beginning to overtake her, and she murmured desperately under his kiss.

Unaccountably, she had flashing vision of the hawk striking the little bird, and with a small cry, she mustered her determination. She pushed hard against Ren's shoulders, and turned her face away from his kiss. Her cheek lay against his shoulder, and she felt the soft cotton against her skin and inhaled his warm, clean scent.

Ren held her gently, without speaking. She could hear his rapid heart beat, and then wondered if perhaps it was her own, instead. It would be so easy, the thought came floating up, to just give herself over to him, and to let herself be carried away by the current of her need.

But...his arrogance and presumption, she reminded herself. She would not allow herself to surrender to this desire to let him have his way with her.

Mustering her strength and determination, she pushed herself away from his hard, muscled body, and willed her eyes to clear.

"Let me go," she hissed. "You have no right."

"Don't I?" Ren murmured, looking her over with heated, roving eyes.

"No, you do not," said Nicole, hoping that her voice sounded firm.

"Then, give me that right, Nicole."

She took a small half-step to turn away from him, but could not will herself to take another. "I don't want this," she heard herself saying as she turned back to him.

"Don't you?" Ren replied softly.

He took her in his arms once more, and this time, he opened her mouth with his kiss. Nicole was galvanized by the sensation of need that coursed through her body. She allowed him to pull her to him so close that she could feel his hard thighs against her, and his flat, tight abdomen.

Nicole raised her arms and held Ren desperately, feeling her full breasts flatten against his muscled chest. She heard with satisfaction his groan, and then kissed him back with a fire and a need that threatened to consume her. Time stretched and melted in the heat of her heightening desire. Never had she imagined the power in the flood of sensation that engulfed her.

This time, it was Ren who pulled away, gently but decisively. Nicole opened her eyes, confused.

"I'd better go," he said softly.

Nicole stood, looking off into the green blur of vegetation. As her breathing slowed and her skin began to cool, she felt desperation and anger rise to wash away the heat of her need. Ren had forced from her a response she had never imagined, and now he had left her standing under the trees with an aching, unfulfilled anguish.

The man had no scruples, she thought angrily. Each and every meeting she had had with Ren ended with her feeling foolish, and confused, or distraught in some other way. It was as if he deliberately was toying with her, and enjoying her increasing confusion.

Most distressing of all the unhappy, unsettling feelings he provoked in Nicole was the strange way she had felt so powerless and weak against his body, and so eager for their kiss to continue. It had been Ren, not her, who had ended their embrace and walked away, Nicole reminded herself with humiliation. She clenched her fists by her side and bit her lip, willing herself not to cry. She looked through the trees in the direction of the Cypress Retreat, and wondered how she was going to be able to face Allen and Aunt Jane in her state of emotional disarray. Nicole looked up into the trees as if seeking some strength and solace in the leafy canopy of green. A lizard rested on a low branch overhead, expanding the ruby-red sack on the underside of its neck. It was larger than the familiar chameleons in her Naples garden. A bird called out, and the lizard scampered up the trunk of the tree.

Nicole headed up the path to the Cypress Retreat.

Chapter 6

Nicole slipped in to the Cypress Retreat through the door at the end of the corridor where her room was located. She took a few minutes to wash her face and neck, and to brush out her hair. As she retied it at the nape of her neck, she examined her reflection in the mirror. Her eyes wee serious and dark.

After a few more moments, Nicole gathered her courage and made her way down the hall to join Allen and her Aunt on the screened porch, where they were drinking lemonade. Allen stood as she entered, and pulled out a chair for her at the table.

"Have some lemonade with us," he invited.

"Thanks, I'd love some," Nicole said, seating herself. "How are you doing?" she asked her aunt.

"Well enough. I've been writing out some bills," she replied.

Allen grimaced. "That's a part of business that I'm none too fond of."

"Well, they have to be paid," said Aunt Jane, "so I just do it."

"Marta, my assistant, does most of ours," Allen commented, "for which I am grateful."

Nicole was silent. Allen looked at her, and then cleared his throat. Nicole looked down at her lemonade glass.

"I have some news I forgot to share with you," he said. "There's a fabulous, end-of-the-season party that the gallery is going to put on soon at a wonderful, Gulf-front home. Marta will be coordinating much of it, but your special touches will be most welcome."

Nicole smiled a little wanly. "Sounds like fun," she replied.

"I hope so," Allen said. "It'll be our last big event, to close out the season."

Aunt Jane asked to excuse herself and went off into the lodge, heading toward the kitchen.

"So." Allen said.

Nicole looked at him soberly.

"Speaking of parties, there is going to be a small, but nice, affair tomorrow night at Ned Fisher's."

"The collector?" Nicole asked. "He was in a couple of weeks ago, asking about Egyptian artifacts, of all things. I didn't know how to help him, so I referred him to Marta."

"She told me," Allen nodded. "Would you like to go?"

"Go back to Naples tomorrow?" Nicole asked.

"Yes."

Nicole took a deep breath. "Yes, I believe I would."

Allen looked relieved. "Great!" He said. "You can bring back your painting and anything else you might have been working on. You really should begin to get prepared for a show, soon. I'd love to help you get yourself established as an artist."

Nicole was silent.

"Is something wrong?" Allen inquired. His eyes were on her. Nicole looked away. She would have to say something.

"Sounds nice," she said, finally. "I hope I'm ready for a show. I don't feel I've

been very productive since I left school."

Allen smiled encouragingly. "It doesn't have to be a major event, yet. Now that you're used to the routine at the gallery, you should make some time to get ready. I know you don't have much room to spare at your apartment. Feel free, anytime, to use some of the space at the gallery to work. We have that back storage room—it has a couple of skylights, so the light should be fine for painting."

"Thanks!" replied Nicole. "That's a nice offer."

"Great!" said Allen. "It's at your disposal, then."

Nicole looked at Allen, smiling slightly. He was, indeed, a friend.

Aunt Jane returned, wiping her hands on her apron. "More lemonade, anyone?"

"Please," said Allen.

"None for me right now, thanks," said Nicole.

Aunt Jane poured Allen and herself each a glass and sat down at the table with them.

"How are you two doing?" she asked, looking at Allen.

"Well, thanks," replied Allen. "Nicole and I were just talking about some plans to get her some space to paint at the gallery."

"That's nice," commented Jane.

"I've also invited her to a party back in Naples tomorrow night."

Aunt Jane looked at Nicole questioningly.

"Yes," said Nicole. "I have to be back at work Monday, anyway."

"Of course you do," Aunt Jane nodded. "I sure will miss you, though."

"I'll miss you, too."

"I hope you'll be back soon."

Nicole felt a pang of sharp concern. How would she be able to continue to visit her aunt and still manage to be sure that she wouldn't run into Ren Steele? Her brow was furrowed as she responded carefully. "I'll be back. We'll talk about when later, after I figure some things out."

Her aunt was silent. Finally, she turned to Allen and said casually, "I hope we'll be seeing you, again at some point, too. Maybe we can figure out, if we spend some more time at it, if we know any body in common. you'd be amazed at the diverse people who eventually find their way out here."

Allen smiled tightly. "It's a small world."

"So they say," retorted Aunt Jane. Her smile was surprisingly bleak, thought Nicole. Possibly it was her own disturbed state of mind that was coloring her perceptions.

"Is it possible," asked Allen politely, "that there would be some place here where I could do an hour's work before too long? I have some business calls to make and some emails to send."

"No problem," said Aunt Jane. "You're welcome to use our office. The desk is a little messy, but I am move aside some things to make room for you."

"Don't trouble yourself," Allen said. "I really won't need any thing special, just a chair and a little corner of a desk or table."

He followed her into the Cypress Retreat's business office. There was a cluttered oak desk, a couple of two-drawer file cabinets, and a bookshelf stacked with piles of office supplies. A curtain-less floor-to-ceiling window looked out into the woods behind the lodge.

"This is perfect," Allen said. "Let me just go get my laptop."

He returned a few minutes later carrying a slim, gray plastic case and set it on the desk. He opened it to expose the screen and keyboard, and turned it on. The computer beeped quietly, and the familiar colored operating system logo appeared on the screen.

"Isn't that something?" remarked Aunt Jane. "I didn't know that you didn't have to

plug those things in."

"I'm using my cell phone as a "hot spot" for the WiFi."

"Well, I'll leave you to do your work."

"Thank you. And thanks again for our hospitality. I truly appreciate you allowing me to visit." He paused. "Nicole means a lot to me, you know."

"She means a lot to me, too," said Aunt Jane evenly. "She's talked about how much she enjoys working at your gallery. It sounds like a very interesting business that you have."

"Thank you," said Allen. "It's a pretty good living, and it makes for quite an attractive life-style, I think."

"Nicole seems to like it."

"I hope so," said Allen. "I hope she'll remain with us for a long time."

Nicole was standing, staring off into the woods, when Aunt Jane joined her on the back porch.

"I think I'll take my sketch pad, and go out for a while," she said, turning to her aunt. "Would that be okay with you?"

"Sure. Where were you thinking of going?"

"I don't really know the area. I had been thinking of going up that path we took with Quinn."

Aunt Jane thought for a moment. "Why don't I tell you how to get to Quinn's cabin, instead? He doesn't really talk about it, but he's got quite an interesting place. Around here, we call it the Orchid Farm, and some people call him "Orchid Man.""

"I had no idea," said Nicole. "Orchids? I'd love to see them. Can we call him and ask it its a good time for me to come?"

"No telephone," responded Aunt Jane. "But I can assure you, if he's there, he'd welcome the company, and if he's not there, he wouldn't mind if you looked around as much as you like."

Aunt Jane carefully explained how to find the trail that led to the Orchid Farm and Nicole set out through the woods. She'd liberally sprayed herself with a skin softener reputed to also be an excellent mosquito repellent. The late afternoon sun was casting long shadows, and translucent clouds of mosquitoes hovered beneath the canopy of trees.

After about a twenty-minute walk east along a trail that approximately paralleled the main highway, Nicole came to a large, partially cleared glade. A small cabin was set in the middle of the clearing. Quinn was outside, smoking a pipe, and looking off into the trees.

"Hello, there," called Nicole.

Quinn turned in Nicole's direct and squinted into the sunlight.

"Well, there, Missy," he said, "What brings you out in this direction?"

"Aunt Jane suggested that I might visit. She said you have orchids. I hope its not an inconvenient time."

"No engraved invitation necessary," Quinn said, extending his hand. "Any time's a good time, any time at all."

"Thank you," replied Nicole, looking around. She didn't immediately see any orchids. Stacked somewhat haphazardly off to one side of Quinn's cabin was a pile of small, slatted crates, measuring perhaps eight inches on a side. Some were even smaller, and all were empty. She looked for a green house, and saw nothing resembling one. There was only the cabin, and a small, dark-looking shed.

Quinn watched her eyes, and followed her visual search. "Give up?"

Nicole smiled. "I guess so."

"Look up," he suggested.

Nicole gasped softly. The trees above were filled with hundreds, if not thousands, of gorgeous blooms. Some of the plants were growing in baskets made from the small crates. Others were fastened to flattened slabs of bark or wood that were nailed to trees. Others seemed to grown from the very tree limbs that supported them. Nicole turned slowly, taking in the sheer beauty of the display.

Quinn smiled proudly. "Aren't they something?"

"They sure are," breathed Nicole. "I don't know if I've ever seen a more beautiful sight."

"There are at least 15,000 different species, world wide," said Quinn, looking around, "although I have only about three hundred here. The ones that are growing from the slabs and directly on the trees are mostly epiphytes. They get their nutrients from the air and from decaying organic matter on the tree surfaces. The semi-epiphytes are growing in the boxes. I have a few semi-terrestrials, too."

"Are they much trouble to grow?" asked Nicole.

"Not much trouble at all, around here," replied Quinn. "The natural conditions here of temperature, humidity, and light, are pretty much to their liking. They thrive on humidity. The relative humidity around here is usually perfect for them. During the dry season, I have to use a hose to soak the once a week, if it doesn't rain. Actually, the cattleyas and the phalaenopsis, of which I have a lot, need it more often when it's dry. They do far better with just rain water, though."

"I thought they had to be grown in green houses" said Nicole, admiring the blooms of a fuchsia cattleya.

"One of the advantages of growing them like this is the natural ventilation and air circulation," replied Quinn. "In greenhouses, they have to give all manner of attention to air circulation. Out here, it just happens."

"Do they bloom all year around?"

"Well, their peak in South Florida is generally between January and April, so the best of their display is about over for this year."

"All these can't be native to Florida," Nicole wondered aloud.

"Some are, actually," replied Quinn. "See those little numbers wrapped around the tree trunks? No leaves? Some call it palm-polly, and it's a native, for example. But you're right, a lot of what I have, you'd see more of in Central America or Columbia."

Nicole walked slowly among the trees, admiring the diversity of the orchid foliage and blooms. She loved the lushness of the larger, showier blossoms, and was fascinated by the cascading falls of tiny, individual blossoms that graced some of the specimens.

Getting out the sketch book she'd brought along, Nicole drew details of fleshy leaves and delicate blossoms. She made notes on the sketches concerning color and species characteristics. Quinn followed along, adding comments and answering Nicole's questions.

Finally, the light from the setting sun grew too faint to work anymore. Nicole looked around. It would be dark, soon, and she was quite far from the Cypress Retreat.

A footfall on the soft turf caused her to turn around. Ren Steele was just a few yards away. He greeted Quinn with the casual hello of old friends. He nodded briefly at Nicole. She stared at him, momentarily speechless. Had he followed her out here, somehow unobserved? The thought made Nicole furious. She decided to keep her suspicions to herself. This time, she would not, foolishly, allow herself to be provoked. Saying nothing, she turned away, and wandered off near the shed, clutching her sketch book.

Behind her a few yards, Quinn and Ren strolled together. As well as Nicole could determine from what she could overhear, they were talking about fishing.

Nicole decided it would be a good time to make her way back to the Cypress Retreat. The path back was across the clearing. She would have to come around from behind the shed to thank Quinn and to say her goodbyes. "I can manage this," she said firmly to herself.

Head held high and shoulders pulled back, she walked around to where the two men were standing.

"Quinn," she called, "I'll be going now. Thank you for the interesting visit. Your orchids are amazing. I appreciate the time you spent with me."

"Any time, young lady," Quinn said with a small bow. "My pleasure. Come back again, and I'll have some specimens potted up for you to take with you."

"Thank you so much," said Nicole politely.

"Tell your aunt I send my greetings."

"I will" She turned to go.

"I'll walk you back," Ren offered casually.

"That won't be necessary," said Nicole crispy.

"It would be my pleasure," replied Ten. "No trouble at all."

"No thank you, I said."

Ren scowled. Quinn turned his head, trying to hide his smile. "The sun has set. It will be completely dark in a few minutes. You don't know this area."

"How hard can it be to follow the path?" Nicole said defiantly. "I can find my way back without your kind of help."

Quinn laughed out loud, but seeing the blaze of anger in Nicole's eyes, he smothered it. "Mr. Steele's right, Miss Nicole," he said seriously. "The woods at night are no place to be if you don't know the trails. Your aunt would never forgive me if I let you go off by yourself in the dark and anything happened to you."

"I'm sure I'll be perfectly fine," Nicole insisted. She turned to go, and realized how black the swampland had become now that the sun was completely gone. She could no longer see where the trail out of Quinn's clearing began. The prospect of finding her way back to her aunt's lodge in the dark was a little frightening.

Ren, sensing her capitulation, said curtly, "Follow me". He headed off without waiting to see if Nicole was behind him. He slipped into the woods, scarcely making a sound as he threaded his way along the narrow path. Nicole found herself having to walk quickly to keep him in sight. In the dark, the trees seemed to close over her. The last remnants of dusky light had rapidly faded to black. She could no longer see even the ground beneath her feet. She brushed against a sticky spider web, and, despite herself, cried out.

Ren was beside her suddenly. "Here, take my hand," he offered, and Nicole grasped it. "Just put one foot in front of the other," he directed. "The ground is solid. We're going back exactly the same way you came out." With that, he gave Nicole's had a tug, and they started off.

At first, Nicole's steps were hesitant, and she wished Ren would slow down. She did not want to appear foolish or afraid, so she concentrated on her breathing and began to relax. She was reminded of games she'd played as a child, when someone was blindfolded and had to trust that another would lead him safely around a room or a play ground.

After a few more minutes of gliding through the enveloping darkness, her hand securely in Ren's warm clasp, Nicole thought she could see light breaking through the foliage. Eagerly she surged forward. Her toe caught against a tree root, and she would have fallen, but Ren turned back toward her, and her shoulder struck him on the chest.

He pulled her up against him, and then he was kissing her passionately, pulling her even closer, murmuring in his throat. His lips were devouring her and igniting her. Nicole gave up her resistance quickly, and clung to him in the dark, allowing his hands to caress her back and her shoulders. Nicole felt a tightening in her thighs, and moaned softly, her breath coming hotly. Her eyes closed, and she relaxed against him, giving herself fully to the sensations that swept away all her awareness of time.

As if from a very distant place, Nicole heard a voice calling her name. Allen is looking for me, Nicole thought, her body still pressed against Ren's. She opened her eyes, and pushed away from him and turned out of his embrace. She could see the dark shape of a man back lit by the illumination emanating from the grounds of the Cypress Retreat.

"Over here, Allen," called Nicole. Ren cursed softly under his breath. She took a few steps down the trail toward Allen, and the light caught her figure as she smoothed her clothing and hair into place.

"Nicole," Ren said softly, his voice hoarse and low, "don't go to him."

Nicole shook her head, and straightened herself. She walked out into the light and said, "Over here, Allen."

Ren followed her down the trail to the Cypress Retreat and Allen. They stepped out into the circle of light cast downward by a halogen lamp set up on a pole, Ren a few paces behind Nicole, who continued walking toward Allen.

"I was getting a bit worried about you," Allen said. He looked at Ren, and Nicole felt the heat of a flush warm her cheeks. Surely, she looked a mess. She resisted the impulse to tuck in her shirt, not wanting to draw Allen's attention to her loosened clothing.

"I was a Quinn's orchid farm, sketching," Nicole explained. "It got dark more quickly than I expected."

"And Mr. Steele escorted you home. How nice of him," said Allen coolly.

"It wouldn't have been safe for her out in the woods after dark, Ren said.

"Perhaps there are worse things than being along in the woods at night," said Allen crisply, emphasizing the word 'alone'. "Nevertheless, I thank you for seeing to her safe return. Shall we take our leave of M. Steele" he said, addressing himself to Nicole. "Your aunt will be relieved to see you."

Allen offered his arm to Nicole, and she took his elbow with her hand. Together, they walked back toward the rear entrance of the Cypress Retreat.

"I'm sorry you and Aunt Jane were worried," Nicole said with genuine regret. "I'm afraid I lost track of time. I got fascinated, looking at all the orchids," she went on, the enthusiasm rising in her voice. "You should have seen them. There were hundreds, hanging from the trees."

"What about Mr. Steele?" Allen asked a little coldly. "Is he an orchid fancier, as well? He scarcely seems the type."

Nicole laughed merrily, relieved that the awkwardness of the moment appeared to be dissolving. "No, he doesn't seem to be the type, and he's not my type, either," Nicole said more loudly than was necessary. Allen turned back to glance at Ren, and gave Nicole a penetrating, curious look, but said nothing. Nicole went on, unable to stop herself. "He could never be my type."

At the back entrance to the Cypress Retreat, Nicole turned her head, but Ren was nowhere to be seen. She heard a vehicle door slam shut, and the sound of gravel spinning beneath tires.

Nicole shrugged her shoulders.

"Allen," she said impulsively, tugging at his arm, "let's go back to Naples tonight."

Allen looked at her with surprise.

"Tonight? I thought you wanted to stay the night here, and leave tomorrow."

"That's what I'd been thinking, but I really would like to leave now. Besides, we'll be going to that party tomorrow night that you mentioned, and I'll need some time to get unpacked and to look at my mail, and to clean myself up so I look presentable."

"You'd look wonderful if you went just as you are," Allen smiled, "but if you wish to leave tonight, I'm willing. I hope your aunt won't have any hard feelings."

Nicole looked up, startled. She'd been thinking only of herself again, it seemed. "I'll talk to her," she said quietly. "I hope she'll understand."

Nicole was greeted warmly by Fred as she and Allen stepped into the kitchen. Nicole poured herself a glass of water, and drank it down.

"We were getting a little worried about you after it got dark," said Fred. "Allen found you, I see..."

"She was almost home by the time I met her," Allen said.

"Your aunt will be relieved.'

"I figured she'd be okay," said Aunt Jane, coming in to the kitchen. "Quinn would ever let anything happen to her. Here, let me get you two your dinners. You must be starved. I made lasagna."

She set out two plates on the kitchen table. "I hope you don't mind eating out here," she went on. "I've already cleaned up the dining room. Some of the guests are using the tables to play cards. Some of them are playing pinochle, or spades. Some are in from the outside, playing pool in the bar. The Yankees are playing on the TV."

"All kinds of entertainment happening tonight," Fred said jovially.

Nicole smile wanly.

"How did you like the orchids?" asked Fred. "Old Quinn has quite the flower-jungle, doesn't he?"

"They were lovely," said Nicole.

Aunt Jane looked at her shrewdly. "And?"

Nicole shrugged. "They were lovely," she repeated.

"How's Quinn getting along?"

"He was very nice. He told me about orchid culture, and I sketched a few botanical details. He said to say 'hello'."

"Quinn is quite the collector," said Aunt Jane. "He's been written up in the various orchid-culture publications, and from time-to-time, some features writer from the Miami or Tampa paper "discovers" him, and does a story."

"Does he earn a living with the orchids?" asked Nicole.

"Well, he's retired," replied Aunt Jane. "He doesn't really talk much about the selling part of it, just he collecting. You should hear some of the wild yarns he tells about his travels to the Amazon basin and to the mountains of Columbia. Years ago, he says, he used to have a boat that he sailed around the Caribbean. He's had quite the colorful life.

"Sounds fascinating," said Nicole.

"It really doesn't take too much prodding to get him going on his stories, so whenever you want to hear his tales, just go out there and ask him a few questions."

"I'll do that," smiled Nicole. She sighed deeply, and a sad look clouded her features. She would have to talk about leaving the Cypress Retreat; she could no longer put it off.

"Aunt Jane," Nicole began.

"Yes, dear, I'm all ears. What's on your mind?"

Nicole smiled briefly at Aunt Jane's cliche. She took a breath and continued. "I'm thinking of going back to Naples."

"Is that all?" asked Aunt Jane. "I assumed you would be, and soon. You said you have to get back to work, don't you, on Monday?"

"Yes," said Nicole.

"You also said you had been invited to that party tomorrow might.'

Nicole nodded.

Her aunt looked at her with a question in her eyes. When Nicole didn't immediately respond, Aunt Jane nodded. "There's something more."

"Well, yes," said Nicole hesitantly. "I told Allen that I want to go back tonight."

Aunt Jane raised an eyebrow. "Tonight? Isn't it getting late for a trip? Are you sure it wouldn't be better to leave in the morning?"

"That might seem more practical," Nicole admitted, "but I really do want to go back."

"I hate to think of you driving all that way in the dark. It would be so late by the time you got going. It's not like you could just ride with Allen, is it? You both have your cars here. I wish you would reconsider."

"We could work something out with the cars easily enough," said Allen. "We could take either Nicole's or mine, and drive back together. I could send a couple of guys out over the weekend to pick up which ever vehicle we left here."

Fred nodded. "That could work. Or, I could do something similar with a friend on this end."

"I'd hate to put anyone to that much trouble," said Nicole.

"Well, why hot just stay the night, then?" suggested Aunt Jane. "I'm petrified at the idea of you, especially, driving a car to Naples this late. The road back is straight and two-lane, for the most part, and it would be all too easy to fall asleep at the wheel and end up in a drainage ditch, or worse."

"Happens from time to time on this road," Fred added.

Allen looked at Nicole. "What do you want to do? I could drive us back in one of the cars—I feel well-rested and quite alert, really."

"You've had a very long day," Aunt Jane said, looking at Nicole. "I'd feel better if you stayed here over tonight."

Nicole sighed. "I am tired, so it would be best if I didn't drive. But, I really am determined to go back tonight, one way or the other."

"I'll drive," said Allen quickly. ""You wouldn't have to worry," he said to Aunt Jane. "We could take Nicole's car, so she would have something to drive around town, and I could send somebody out tomorrow or Sunday to get mine. If it would be okay to leave it here for a day or two," he added politely.

"Well, if you insist on going tonight, that would be the best way," said Aunt Jane.

"Okay, then," said Nicole, rising "I think I'll take a quick shower, change clothes, and get packed we we can get started before it gets any later."

"Want me to help you pack?" offered Aunt Jane. "I don't want you two to get off any later than necessary."

"Thanks," said Nicole.

As they walked down the long hallway to Nicole's room, Aunt Jane asked casually, "Did something happen tonight that upset you?"

Nicole sighed, and opened her bedroom door. "I know it must seem impulsive or ill-considered of me to want to eave tonight, but I really think it's for the best. Allen's a good driver, and we'll be fine." She knew she wasn't answering her aunt's question.

"Well, whatever it is, I hope it won't keep you from coming back to visit."

Nicole was silent.

"You will be back, won't you?" asked Aunt Jane, busying herself with some of Nicole's packing.

"You really don't have to do that, Aunt Jane," said Nicole, referring to the packing. "Just let me jump in the shower."

Nicole went into the bathroom, peeled off her clothes, wrapped her hair up in a towel, and turned on the shower. The warm spray felt so good on her tired body. She lathered herself up with a bar of lavender-scented soap, and let the suds and water erase the oily, mosquito repellent spray she'd used on her skin. She willed herself not to think of Ren, and, instead, imagined the sense of freedom from care she would feel, driving along the dark road back to Naples.

Aunt Jane was no longer in her room when Nicole stepped out of the bathroom. Her clothes were all neatly packed into her open suitcase, and fresh shorts and a tee-shirt were laid out for her. Nicole felt a pang of remorse for not responding to Aunt Jane's hopeful inquiry about a return visit.

Perhaps Aunt Jane would come to Naples for a visit, instead. But that seemed like such an imposition, on brief reflection. She and Fred had a business to run, and no doubt, a substantial mortgage payment to meet. Nicole sigh heavily, and sat down on the bed. She looked around the room, admiring the décor. She thought of the pleasure she'd felt in her aunt's companionship, and the enjoyment she'd experienced in learning more about the Everglades, the orchids, and the ways and means of her aunt's and Fred's business here in the wilderness.

Suddenly, she was angry with Ren. He had no right to deprive her of her aunt's companionship. She, for her part, would have to take responsibility for finding a successful plan to either avoid him entirely, or to make sure she was never alone with him again.

Nicole's mood was much improved when Aunt Jane returned to the room to see how Nicole was progressing.

She smile at her aunt, and held out her arms to embrace her.

"Thank you so much for the wonderful visit. I'm so glad we've found each other again after all these years. It means a lot to me that we're living not so far apart at all."

"Me, too," said Aunt Jane. "You've grown up to be a wonderful young woman. Your mother and father were so proud of you, and so am I."

"I hope you'll have me back out soon," said Nicole sincerely. She watched her aunt's eyes light up with pleasure.

"Oh, honey, you know you're welcome anytime, the sooner the better."

"Well, said Nicole, "I know it won't be next weekend, but depending on how things go in Naples, I think maybe I could get back here in two or three weekends from now. It would have to be a shorter visit, but the drive isn't really so far."

"That would be nice," said Aunt Jane with satisfaction. "The lodge should get pretty quiet, soon, but I expect it to pick back up in June or July, after school's out. We're going to be booking some families in for the summer. I've got some plans for nature day camp-type activities. I've placed some ads in family-type publications and summer camp periodicals online.

"You're amazing, said Nicole.

"I expect it runs in the family" Aunt Jane retorted, a twinkle in her eyes.

Chapter 7

Nicole an Aunt Jane walked together down the long hallway leading to the Cypress Retreat's great room and entrance foyer. Nicole set down her luggage near the front door. Allen's overnight bag and computer case were already waiting in the foyer. Allen himself was across the room at the bar, watching a soccer match on television with the lounge's other patrons. He seemed to be part of a noisy conversation about one of the player's records from the previous season. Fred was tending bar.

Nicole crossed the room to where Allen was sitting. He smiled at her warmly and then turned back to the television to watch the action.

"I'll be ready in a shake, luv," he said, "as soon if I see if they manage to score."

Nicole wandered across the room, looking for Aunt Jane, who had disappeared. In a moment, Jane came out of the office, and, spying Nicole, said, "Allen has a telephone call. Would you tell him? He can take it in the office."

Nicole looked at her aunt, who shrugged, and turned back to notify Allen of his call.

"Who is it? Why didn't they call my cell phone?" he asked, his eyes still on the action.

"I don't know. Aunt Jane took the call."

Allen stood up, and slowly made his way across the room, pausing to glance back at the soccer action every few steps. When he reached the office, he closed the door.

Aunt Jane and Nicole waited in the foyer for Allen to finish up on the telephone. "The weather should be alright for your drive back," Jane commented, making small talk.

"I suppose so," nodded Nicole absently.

"I hope it's not too long before we get rain. We really need some, to put an end to this awful drought."

"The summer rains should be due," replied Nicole, "shouldn't they?"

"I hope it's a wet summer, with plenty of torrential downfalls. Of course, it would work best for the business if they were mainly at night."

"I hope that's what happens," Nicole said.

"Oh, I almost forgot," Aunt Jane said. "I was going to give you a few family pictures to take back with you. I have them all set out, but I forgot to bring them to you. I'll be back in a shake," she said, as she hurried off.

Nicole was tired of standing. She looked around for some place to sit, and as her glance swept the room, she saw Ren Steele stepping through the door near the bar. Nicole froze. At that moment, Allen came out of the office, a look of contrition on his face.

"I'm sorry I took so long on the telephone," he said.

Nicole barely heard him. Ren Steele was striding across the room purposefully, heading in their direction.

"It was Marta on the telephone," Allen continued. "She was going on and on about something, and I couldn't break away."

Ren had reached them, and when he heard Allen mention Marta's name, he stopped in his tracks and a strange, cynical smile appeared on his face.

"All ready, luv?" Allen asked. "We need to get going right away." He hadn't noticed Ren.

"I'm ready," replied Nicole, ignoring Ren who had stopped a few feet away on pretext of talking with one of the locals. "I'm just waiting for Aunt Jane, who went somewhere to get something."

"I hope she won't be long," said Allen, a trifle anxiously. "I really do need to get back. Marta's all in a state over something."

Nicole shot Ren a look. Again, when he heard Marta's name, his head turned in their direction and his mouth twisted with a the strange smile.

"He knows Marta. The thought came to Nicole out of nowhere. And that funny-looking smile he gets when

Allen says her name...suddenly, Nicole was certain that there was some connection between the beautiful Marta and Ren. Perhaps they had dated, or had had an affair. That would explain Ren's connection to the Pelican Gallery, and why he had been at the party the night Nicole had first seen him.

Nicole felt a tightness constricting her throat. It fit! Ren had been—or was—dating Marta. Her first impression of him, that night at the party, had been that he was a wealthy playboy of some type. She might have been closer to the truth with that first impression, at least with respect to the playboy part, than she had imagined.

Suddenly, she couldn't bear to be at the lodge a moment longer. Turning to Allen, she said, "Let's put our bags in the car and get going. I don't know what happened to Aunt Jane, but let's find her and Fred, and say goodbye."

Allen shrugged, and picked up his laptop case and Nicole's larger suit case. "I'll just put these in the boot while you see if you can find your aunt."

Nicole hurried off down the hall where she had seen Jane disappear. All the doors were closed, and some of them were to guest rooms. Where had Aunt Jane gone? She considered calling out for her, but she didn't want to risk disturbing any of the guests who might be sleeping already. She started to turn back, but then Aunt Jane appeared from behind one of the doors, caring a cardboard box.

"Sorry this took a while," said Aunt Jane. "I packed in some of your mother's graduation and wedding photos, some of us as children, and our grandfather's Army discharge papers and campaign medals from the war. I also found some ribbons your mother had sent me that she won in various rose shows. Sorry I took so long," she said, noting Nicole's anxious face. "Is Allen in that much of a hurry?"

"He's waiting outside," Nicole said distractedly. "I guess we're both in a hurry. Allen got a telephone call—the one you took—and it seems something has come up."

"Trouble?"

"I don't know. He didn't tell me the details."

Nicole took the box of family memorabilia from her aunt. "Thank you for putting these things together for me. I know I'll enjoy looking through them."

"Well, call me if you have any questions about them. I made notes on the backs of the pictures so you should be able to get an idea about who is in them, and the dates."

"Thank you," Nicole said again.

She paused as they neared the end of the hall, and looked about anxiously. She exhaled in relief when she didn't see Ren. Instead, Fred was there, waiting to walk with them to Allen's car.

"Let me take that for you," he said, holding out his bands for the box.

"Thank you," she said., I'll just get the last of our bags." "Already done," said Fred. "Car's all loaded up."

Nicole, Fred, and Jane walked outside. The warm, humid air was still, and the sky was partly cloudy. The moon had risen, and it was already high. It illuminated the patchy clouds against the darkness of the night sky.

"Looks like a nice night," commented Fred.

"It would be a nicer night if we get that rain that we need," said Jane. "Except for the driving part," she added hastily. "I wouldn't want you two driving in the rain, or at least, not in the kind of downpour that we've been hoping for."

"Well, it'll happen when it happens," said Fred philosophically.

"All set?" asked Allen, getting out of the car. The engine was running. He came around to open the passenger door for Nicole.

Nicole turned to Jane and Fred, and gave them each a quick hug. "Thank you so much," she said. "I'll be in touch soon. It has meant so much to me to have reconnected with you."

"You drive safe, now," Fred said to Allen.

"I'll take good care of her," Allen promised.

Nicole got into the passenger seat of her car, shut the door, and lowered the window. As Allen pulled the care around and headed down the driveway to the main road, Nicole turned and waved back at Aunt Jane and Fred.

"We're off," said Allen. Nicole detected relief in his voice.

****

Jane and Red stood together in the darkness by the side of the road, watching as the taillights of Nicole's car disappeared when Allen made the turn west onto the main highway. Fred put his arm around Aunt Jane's shoulders, and pulled her a little close.

"Feeling sad now that she's gone?" asked Fred.

"Sure I am," replied Jane. She's just a wonderful girl isn't she? Looks exactly like her mother did at that age."

"Nicole's a fine young woman," Fred nodded. "Even Quinn spoke highly of her, and, you know he's a man with precious few compliments to spare."

"I sure hope she'll be back," sighed Aunt Jane as she and Fred turned and began to stroll back up the long driveway together.

"Why wouldn't she?" asked Fred. "She said she'd come back, didn't she?"

"Yes, she did," admitted Jane. "She said in two or three weeks—maybe. It's the 'maybe' part that has me a little worried."

"Don't make cares and woes for yourself out of nothing, dear girl," Fred chuckled, fondly patting Aunt Jane's back soothingly.

The two of them stood for a time outside the main entrance of the Cypress Retreat. Fred lit a pipe, and motioned for Jane to sit beside him on a nearby bench.

"Listen to those peepers," he said, exhaling a puff of pungent, sweet-smelling smoke.

"I'm troubling over something I can't quite put my finger on." Jane paused, searching for the words to continue. He took out his pipe tool, and busied himself with relighting the tobacco to his satisfaction.

"Well, what's it got to do with?" he inquired finally. "Worried about the business?'

"No, no more so than usual. It's nothing like that," responded Jane. "It's about Nicole."

Fred looked at Jane. "She seemed like she was doing fine, to me. A wonderful young woman."

"She is, isn't she?" nodded Jane. "Come to think of it, it's not really Nicole who has me concerned. It's that Allen."

"Oh?" replied Fred, his eyebrows raised in surprised. "How do you mean?"

"Well, that's the part I'm having the trouble about,' said Aunt Jane slowly. "At this point, it's nothing too specific. Just a feeling I get."

"What kind of a feeling is it?" Fred pursued gently, looking off into the night. He took another draw on his pipe, and then tapped the ashes out against the bench.

"Make sure those ashes are cold," admonished Jane. "The last thing we need around here would be a brush fire, dry as it's been."

"They're completely out," reassured Fred, grinding them under his heel. "Now, you were saying, what's on your mind?"

"Well, do you remember the Hendersons? They were here in February. From Toronto?"

Fred looked at Jane blankly.

"Oh, you remember," she pursued. "She insisted she wanted to go out and see some alligators, and when you got ready to take her down to the boats, she was dressed in pink leggings and the high-heeled sandals?"

"Oh, yes, yes," smiled Fred. "But they turned out to be quite a nice couple."

"Yes," nodded Jane. "Well," she went on, "I talked to them today."

"Oh?" Fred's eyebrows rose.

"Yes."

"Are they coming back again, so soon?"

"No. I called them."

"In Toronto?" Fred's eyebrows rose higher.

"I called them because I just felt I had to," Jane continued. "Remember the other day at lunch with Allen and Nicole, when were were trying to sort out if we knew anybody he knew from Canada?"

Fred nodded.

"Well, it seems like we do."

"The Hendersons?"

"Yes, the Hendersons. They know of him, anyway, from when he was in Canada."

"And" asked Fred.

"Well, its strange, don't you think, that Allen didn't say anything about it?"

Fred thought for a moment. "No," he said finally, "I don't think it's strange at all. You never asked him about the Hendersons, as I recollect. You mentioned a few names, but nothing about the Hendersons came up."

Jane considered this. "I guess you're right. But he wasn't too interested in the discussion, as I recall."

Fred shrugged.

"I suppose you think I'm trying to make something out of nothing," Jane said.

Fred turned to her and smiled.

"You don't have to say anything," Jane went on. "I know how you think."

Fred stood, and held out his hand to Jane. "Ready to go back in?"

Jane rose from the bench, and walked with Fred into the lodge.

"You might think I'm crazy," she said, "but I asked the Hendersons to let me know if they thought of anything about Allen that we might want to know."

You are being a mite over-protective, I guess, but I wouldn't say that I think you're quite crazy. Not that there's anything wrong with being careful," Fred added hastily, seeing the expression on Jane's face. "I just don't like it when you worry."

****

Allen and Nicole sped east along Highway 41, Allen expertly handling Nicole's car. There was very little traffic late on the Friday night heading in the same direction they were traveling, but there was quite a flow of cars and trucks coming across from the Gulf coast.

Allen lowered the driver's side window and rested his left elbow on the window frame. The breeze lifted strands of Nicole's long hair from the back of her neck. Allen turned on the CD player. Cool jazz filled the car.

"Miles Davis," he said.

Nicole settled into her seat, and closed her eyes. Tonight, she thought, she'd be sleeping in her own bed again. The days she had spent in others' company would be quite a contrast to the weekend ahead. Other than the small get-together Allen had mentioned, Nicole would be alone, to think her own thoughts and to fill her time as she pleased.

"Look," Allen said suddenly. Nicole opened her eyes, and looked around but saw nothing. The traffic had thinned, and they were alone on this stretch of road.

"What?" she asked

"You missed it. It was an armadillo or something, that went trotting across the road. Rather too slowly for its own good, if you ask me, but it got across safely."

"We might see raccoon or 'possums, too," Nicole commented.

"Any deer?""What about those little deer they have down in the Keys? Any of them get up this far?"

"i don't think so. I think they're all confined to just a few of islands that have fresh water. They're a special subspecies, I think, None up here."

Nicole settled back again and closed her eyes. She listened to the soft music and the sound of the tires on the highway, and her breathing slowed. She felt warm and safe in the darkness with Allen.

"We'll be having that party for the gallery soon," Allen said. "I hope it goes well."

"How much is left to do?" Nicole asked sleepily.

"Well, the invitations went out all right, and the place we're having it is quite nice. Marta's been looking after most of the details."

"Is that what she called about?" Nicole asked.

Allen was silent. Finally, he said, "not really. She had something else on her mind."

"Oh?" responded Nicole. Allen didn't provide any more information, though, and Nicole's thoughts drifted. She thought of the air boat ride she had taken, and as her car flew along the dark highway, Nicole imagined herself skimming over the surface of the Everglades' waterways. She thought of Fred with his placid equanimity, and how he and Jane seemed to complement each other so well. They were probably both asleep by now, being soothed by the chorus of night sounds produced by the frogs and insects.

She thought of Ren, and wondered if he, too, was asleep. Where did he spend his nights? Did he have a cabin somewhere? Was he alone?

Nicole stirred in her seat.

"Comfortable?" Allen asked.

"I'm okay," replied Nicole. She didn't want to think about Ren anymore. She didn't want to think about

Marta's telephone all. She didn't want to revisit her impulsive and ridiculous-seeming assumption that Ren and Marta knew each other. Nicole, relaxed and on her way home, was sure now that she had leapt to an illogical conclusion back at the lodge. Besides, even if they did know each other, it was of no concern to her. Nicole did not consider Marta to be friend, so there was no reason for their paths to cross outside of the purely business dealings. And, she had no interest at all in entertaining further speculations about Ren. The passing miles had emboldened her. She was quite sure she could manage to avoid Ren Steele effectively back in Naples. Perhaps she would even confide in Aunt Jane how much she disliked him, and Aunt Jane could help make sure she did not run into him the next time she visited the Cypress Retreat. Nicole smiled to herself, enjoying the feelings of certainty and confidence she feel growing as the car sped along.

There would be no need, ever again, for her to be vulnerable to Ren Steele and to his unwanted advances. Nicole felt quite sure that she had done nothing improper to give Mr. Steele the impression that she would welcome his love-making. He was simply an opportunist, and so arrogant and sure of himself that he had assumed he could take advantage of Nicole's inexperience and uncertainties. Now that she knew what kind of a man he was, she would be better-prepared to handle herself in the unlikely event that she couldn't avoid him completely.

"Penny for your thoughts," Allen said.

Nicole opened her eyes. They were passing through a small, unincorporated area east of Naples. Soon they would be home. She looked over at Allen, and smiled. "It's good to be getting back. I'm looking forward to coming in to work on Monday."

"I'm relieved to hear you say that. For a time there, I'd been getting worried that you might have been beginning to grow some roots back there in the swamp."

Nicole's smile broadened. "Not so. I had a nice couple of days visiting with my Aunt, who I love dearly, but there are absolutely no roots sprouting from these sandals."

Allen laughed warmly. "You don't know how glad I am to hear you say those words," he reiterated. "I had been entertaining the thought that you might not be coming back to us."

Nicole looked over at him in surprise. "How could you think such a thing?"

Allen shrugged. "I don't know, luv. You sounded as if you were so taken with your aunt and her tourist business that I thought you might decide to stay on."

"Stay on? But, my job at the gallery...my apartment..." Nicole ran out of words, so shocked was she by what Allen had said. How could he have imagined that she would leave the Pelican without even giving proper notice?

"Stranger things have happened," he said. "I thought perhaps your aunt might offer you work with her."

"The subject never came up," replied Nicole, still amazed at what Allen was saying.

"I'm highly relieved," he said. "I've been doing some thinking, you know. I hope very much that I can interest you I an expanded role with us, at the gallery."

"What kind of a role?" asked Nicole, her curiosity piqued.

"I haven't worked it all out, yet. I'm still considering the various options. More of a partnership role, perhaps."

"Partnership?" Nicole was confused. "I don't know what your mean. When I hear the word 'partnership', I think of shared assets. At least, that's what I learned in my business classes. I certainly don't have the capital or the expertise to be a partner."

"There are other kinds of partnerships," Allen smiled. He took his right hand from the steering wheel and placed it over Nicole's and squeezed it warmly.

What was Allen trying to convey to her? Nicole wondered if he was implying an interest in marrying her. There had been his remark, while they had been walking in the woods, about honeymoon cruises. Nicole frowned. And, there had been something else he had said on that walk that seemed it fit, too, but then, Ren had appeared. Nicole shook her head. "No," she said aloud, willing thoughts of Ren out of her mind.

"No?" Allen question, sounding perplexed.

"No, I didn't mean 'no' to you, I was thinking of something else."

"Go on," Allen invited.

"It's nothing," replied Nicole. "I'm sorry. I just sort of drifted there, for a minute."

Allen sighed. "You're tired. Now is not the time for this discussion. I'd just like to say that I care for you very much, and I'm very happy that you're here with me."

Nicole smiled. They had arrived in Naples proper, and in a few more minutes, Allen turned on to Nicole's street and parked her car safely at her apartment building.

"Let me walk you in," he said, getting her bags out of the trunk.

The street was utterly still. A light from a second floor window of one of the apartments glowed a warm yellow from behind a shade. Nicole stretched and inhaled the humid air. She unlocked her courtyard gate. Allen followed, carrying her bags inside. He set them down by the door and waited while Nicole found the right key to let them in to the apartment.

She turned on the foyer light, and stepped inside. Looking around, she determined that everything was as she had left it.

"I'm thirsty," she said to Allen. "Would you like a glass of ice water?"

"I'd love one," he said. "Mind if I use the lavatory?"

"Go right ahead," she replied.

Nicole carried her luggage into her bedroom. She could wait until tomorrow to unpack. All she wanted now was a nice, hot shower and a good night's sleep in her own bed. She turned on her ceiling fan, and opened the bedroom window. She listened, and heard a faint buzz of insects against the window screen. The night was much quieter than in the Everglades, which had vibrated and pulsed with the sounds of the swamp life.

Allen came out of the bathroom, holding his glass of ice water. He drained it, and set it down on Nicole's dresser.

"You know," she said, "you can take my car home tonight. That would be best, don't you think?"

"If you say so, my dear," he said with a small shrug. "I can have it back to you in the morning, no problem."

"That would be fine," Nicole said.

"Well, I'll be off, then."

Nicole walked with Allen to her front door, and followed him out into the courtyard.

"Good night. Drive safely."

"You know I will."

He turned to her, and took her in his arms. He kissed her warmly on the lips. Nicole, taken completely by surprise, held still for a moment, feeling his mouth move softly on hers. Allen's eyes were closed, but Nicole's remain open. She felt tense and uncomfortable in his embrace, and was relieved when he opened his eyes and stepped back. He regarded with a question in his eyes. Nicole dropped her gaze.

"Well," he said finally, "i guess I'll be off. I'll call you about the party. Your car should be back not too late tomorrow."

"Thank you," Nicole said quietly. "Good night."

After Nicole had showered and washed her hair, she put on a long cotton gown. She took her hair brush and a glass of ice water outside to her courtyard, and sat down at her patio table. A breeze had come up, and Nicole began to brush out her long hair. She lifted each section, and drew the brush through it for several strokes, feeling the drops of moisture that settled coolly on her bare shoulders. She enjoyed feeling her scalp tingle, and the fresh feeling of being clean from the shower.

Nicole's thoughts tuned to what had just happened between her and Allen. It seemed he was beginning to become interested in her as something more than just an employee and a friend, and Nicole needed now to sort out just how she felt about his attentions.

Allen was polite, good-humored, attractive, and quite well-off financially. They shared an interest in art and business, and she had regarded him as a trustworthy, supportive friend and mentor. But, never had she thought of him as a potential romantic partner. Nicole had not been one to mix romance and employment. Although, she conceded to herself, she really hadn't understood that workplace romances were fairly commonplace.

Nicole thought about the kiss, and wondered at her lack of responsiveness, True, she had been taken by surprise and was also very tired from the long day. Still, she had been curiously detached and unmoved by his embrace.

Nicole sighed. Allen could be a very suitable partner for her. Unlike Ren, he was well-mannered, sensitive to her feelings, and interested in her welfare. But, she would be terribly dishonest with herself if she denied the exciting, overpowering feelings she had experienced in Ren's embraces. His arrogant way with her angered her intensely, but never had she experienced anything like the sensations aroused by his kisses. She closed her eyes, remembering how her skin had tingled as his lips had moved on her neck, and how her arms had clung desperately to him as she had pressed herself against his hard, muscled flesh. And, the fire that had been ignited deep within her as his hands had caressed her body had disturbed her terribly, but now seemed in vivid contrast to the cool detachment she had felt in Allen's arms.

Nicole sighed again. She got up, and slowly crossed the patio. Inside her apartment, she turned off the lights after carefully locking the doors, and got into bed. Her sheets felt cool and smooth. The ceiling fan over the bed softly stirred the air in the room. She listened to the sounds of the breeze rustling and shivering the long fronds of the palm trees growing outside her window.

Allen seemed safe and warm. Ren was disturbing, and somehow dangerous. Allen had talked of a partnership. Ren toyed with her, and kept her off balance. Never, did she feel safe with him.

Sleepily, Nicole remembered being led through the dark woods at night, holding tightly to Ren's hand. She had relaxed eventually, and had allowed him to lead her safely back to the Cypress Retreat. Nicole stirred, and turned over beneath her sheet. She had had no choice then but to have submitted to his leadership. He knew the woods, and she would have been utterly lost without him.

But, surely, there were more important bases for a relationship than exciting kisses. She hadn't really given Allen a chance. Over time, now that she was beginning to think of Allen in a new light, she might find herself more open and responsive to his love-making. And, now that she was back in Naples, she could push en Steele out of her thoughts, and give herself a chance to forget all about him.

Chapter 8

Monday morning dawned cloudy and humid. Nicole turned of her alarm clock, and pulled her covers up to her chin. She stretched her legs, and contemplated falling back to sleep for another two hours. After just a few short minutes, however, she sat up in bed. Aunt Jane would have been up for quite a while by now, seeing to the Cypress Retreat's guests, and helping them to arrange their activities for the day. Nicole had called her aunt to let her know that she had arrived back in Naples safely. Their conversation had been brief; Aunt Jane was making preparations to take some birders out canoeing.

Nicole got out of bed, and, as was her habit, she opened all the curtains and blinds in the apartment to let light spill into her rooms. She poured herself a cup of coffee and laid out her work clothes.

She dressed carefully, and settled on her mother's pearl necklace and small gold hoop earrings. She twisted her hair into an arrangement at the back of her head, and secured it with two long ebony pins. The effect was slightly oriental.

After a quick breakfast, Nicole took her mug of coffee out to her car. As she drove along the boulevard, she wondered what her day ahead at the Pelican Gallery would hold. She felt eager to get back to work, but a little concerned about the state of some of her projects. Nicole shrugged to herself; she would just have to work extra hard to get herself back up to speed.

Millie greeted her warmly and handed her a stack of messages. Nicole took her coffee to her desk, and began to plan her wok day. She had several calls to return from customers, and some publicity materials to review and edit. The printer had returned a stack of fliers to be mailed out to the Pelican's customer list announcing future shows. A new framing supplier had dropped off samples in the latest materials and color selections, and was offering to set up a display of his line at the gallery. Nicole made a note to call him to ask for referrals for the consignment services of custom framers. The young man who did the Pelican's framing during the winter season would be leaving to go north for the summer to work in a Provincetown gallery until mid-October.

At ten o'clock, two women, a daughter and her elderly mother, came in to look at some art. Nicole introduced herself, and offered to show them the gallery's current offerings.

"I'm looking for a large, framed print of some type to hang over my buffet in the dining room," began Mrs. Carter. "My husband, bless his soul, couldn't abide contemporary art, and, consequently, our home is hung with godawful dark oils. Some of them are quite fine, actually, but I can't stand the stuff, personally. When we were living in New Hampshire in the farm house that had been in his family since the 1840's, I didn't mind so much, but down here in Florida, none of it looks right in the condominium. Do you sell by consignment, or could you recommend a good auction house? I can't wait to get rid of the oils."

Nicole promised to consult with Allen, after taking the woman's name and telephone number. Meanwhile, Mrs. Carter's daughter, a small woman in her forties with dark bangs and horn-rimmed glasses, had found some of Robin Sloane' bird lithographs.

"Look at these, mother. What do you think?"

"Birds. Ugh," snapped Mrs. Carter. "Every old biddie in the Palm Pavilion has seagulls and pelicans on their walls. If I want to look at birds, I'll go down to the beach. I want something colorful and abstract. Something your father, and his father, and the entire line of Carters all the way back to the Revolutionary War would have hated. I put up with an old house filled with antiques from cellar to attic for over forty years, and now it's my turn to choose what I want to live with. I want something that would make all those stuffy Carters turn in their graves."

"Mother!"

"Well, I do, Mary Beth. Show us something shocking," she said, turning to Nicole.

"Well," began Nicole hesitantly, "we have some tasteful nudes by a Ft Myers artist who has been gaining quite a following."

"I didn't mean 'shocking' in that sense, young lady. I meant bold and colorful."

Nicole smiled. She led the two women to some good-sized geometric lithographs designed to create stunning optical effects. "These are by Vasarely, who has been called the father of Op Art."

The older woman regarded them solemnly, and nodded. "They sort of hurt your eyes, almost don't they?" She turned to her daughter. "What do you think of that one for the dining room?"

The daughter shrugged. "I don't know, Mother. It's not like anything you've ever had before."

"Good. I'll take it," she said, turning to Nicole. "It ought to make the entire Wednesday morning bridge club call their ophthalmologists."

At lunchtime, Nicole strolled down to a small park two blocks from the gallery, munching on a bagel with cream cheese and sipping a diet cola. She sat for a time in the shade of an old magnolia tree and watched as a pair of mocking birds chased a marauding blue jay out of their territory. Th jay shrieked in protest from the top of a tall light pole. She watched as an old man tapped a long white cane from side to side on a paved walkway, leading a small poodle on a turquoise leash.

The well-groomed park, and the manicured lawns and landscaping of Naples' residential neighborhoods were strikingly in contrast to the wild lushness of the tangle of native trees and shrubs at Aunt Jane's Cypress Retreat. Nicole wasn't really sure which setting she preferred, from an aesthetic point of view. The stands of towering palm trees, some leaning slightly with their long, graceful, rustling fronds hanging almost to the ground, and some with bushy crowns of shorter fronds, were lovely, certainly. Many of the Naples gardens were planted with azaleas and other flowering shrubs banked in beds beneath groups of palm trees, with whole areas nicely mulched with shredded cypress bark and planted in the cooler winter months with colorful annuals.

Nicole also liked living close to the Gulf of Mexico. Walking the beaches at sunset, as the sky turned pink and then purple, watching long-legged white shore birds stalking their suppers as the warm, shallow water receded with the evening ebb tide, was pure bliss. She envisioned herself driving her car to a favorite beach soon, perhaps some evening right after work this week.

She wondered if Ren cared much for beaches, and where he stayed when he was in town. There was a great deal she did not know about Ren Steele, she reflected. Catching herself, she reminded herself firmly that she had decided not to think of him. She had done an excellent job of pushing thoughts of him out of her mind over the weekend, and she would continue to persevere in doing so until his image was completely banished from her day-to-day existence. She would go on with her life in Naples, and each day, he would recede father and farther, leaving her life like an outgoing tide.

Nicole rose, and brushed off her skirt. She deposited her trash in a nearby barrel, and began the short walk back to the Pelican Gallery. I can do this, she pledged. I can enjoy my days at work. I can develop my artistic interests. I can stroll the shore line at sunset. I can rent a catamaran and learn to sail. I can fill my days and nights, and keep pushing out unwanted thoughts and images until I am at peace with myself again. She straightened her shoulders, slung the strap of her bag over her shoulder, and picked up her pace. It was almost one o'clock, and she had a meeting scheduled with Allen.

Nicole stepped in to Allen's office promptly at one. He was seated at his desk, his chair swiveled to face his window, and was talking on the telephone. Nicole noticed a suitcase and his briefcase standing just inside the door. When he saw her, he motioned for her to take a seat on the couch. His smile was distracted.

When he was finished with his call, he turned his chair to face Nicole. "Let me be brief," he began. "I have to catch one of those little commuter planes, shortly. How is your day going?"

"Well enough," Nicole said simply.

"Busy?"

"I have plenty to do," Nicole replied.

"Well, I'm afraid that I'm going to have to ask you to take on a bit more," he said apologetically. "I'm about to leave for Sarasota, and I need your help."

"Of course," replied Nicole.

"There's a bit of urgent business in Sarasota, and I'm not entirely sure how long I'll be gone. I may have to travel to Orlando, or to Miami, or perhaps to both, over the next few days."

Nicole nodded.

"Some details are not going so smoothly with a deal related to some artifacts."

"Artifacts?"

"Mayan, Toltec, Aztec."

Nicole raised her eyebrows, but Allen didn't provide more information.

"There's two areas I want you to concentrate on while I'm gone," Allen continued. "First, I need you to basically take on the running of the gallery. Millie will of course open up, but I need you to stay until closing, and to work on Saturday, as well. Things should go smoothly. Millie will continue to do the billing and accounts receivable. Marta will sign the checks. She'll be in and out quite a bit, but she should be able to answer most of your questions. I'll call in at least once a day." Nicole nodded. So far, Allen didn't seem to be asking much more from her than she usually did, other than working some extended hours and closing up the gallery at the end of the business day, which she had done before.

"I think I can handle that much," Nicole said cheerfully.

"Good," nodded Allen.

"Anything else?" asked Nicole.

"Well, yes," said Allen. "I hate to have to ask you, but I'm going to need you to be in charge of coordinating our end-of-season party at the Mer d'Azur.

Nicole was speechless. The party was a week from Saturday, and was to be the Pelican's biggest, and final, event of the season.

"What has been done so far?" asked Nicole. She had been well-aware of the party, and that some of the preparations had been ongoing but she had really paid no heed to any of the details. She had planned on attending, of course, and had assumed she would be helping in some way, perhaps in the capacity that she had at some of the Pelican's openings, but on a larger scale.

"A fair amount," replied Allen. "It's all on schedule, so far. The invitations were mailed. Millie is handling RSVP and is keeping track of the numbers. The rooms at the villa were reserved, or course. The caterer has been selected."

"What's left to be done, then?" asked Nicole.

"All the rest," replied Allen. "I need you to select the hors d'ouvres and the food from the menu options the caterer has offered within our budget. You'll need to order the wine and drinks from one of the local suppliers— Millie has some names and the budget figures after you have a better idea as to how many will be attending. I want you to familiarize yourself with the guest list, and work with Marta to learn something about the attendees so you can function as a hostess with her. You'll need to go out to the Mer d'Azure to take a look at the rooms so you can decide what to order for flowers and decorations. Music. Gallery brochures. Hang a selection of the Pelican's art...originals only, I think.

Allen paused as Nicole finished jotting some notes. "Sound like fun?" he asked, with a twinkle.

"I'm not sure," responded Nicole slowly, "that I can handle so much for such an important event."

"I'll call in often to see how you're getting on," promised Allen. "I know its more than you're accustomed to doing, but, really, I'm sure you'll find it's mainly in the details. I hope you'll find it enjoyable, actually, and that's really what I hope to provide for our guests—an elegant, enjoyable evening, so that they remember us over the summer and talk about us with potential patrons and customers. I'd like for us to become known as the finest little gallery on the Southwest coast."

Nicole nodded, distracted already from what Allen was saying. What to do first? Perhaps she should plan to go out to the Mer d'Azur to get a look at the place, so she could visualize the facility accurately as she proceeded with making the

arrangements.

"Don't forget, now, luv," Allen was saying. "Marta's taken care of the guest list, and a bit of the rest of it. When you're making your calls, mention her name, as the caterers and so forth have already had contact with her. I'm sure she'll be a big help to you, if you need her."

"Mmm." responded Nicole noncommittally. She doubted very much that Marta would welcome Nicole's questions. Marta probably would be no more enthusiastic about working with Nicole on this project than she seemed to be about working with Nicole on any level, other than ordering her to carry out her requests. At least, Nicole reflected, that had been her experience with Marta, so far.

"Does Marta know that you're asking me to do this?" asked Nicole.

Allen looked at her in surprise. "Of course, luv. It was her suggestion, actually."

Now it was Nicole's turn to look surprised. Allen didn't appear to notice. He rose and said, "I've got to be off, now. It wouldn't do for me to miss my flight. And, by the way, I have a nice surprise for you."

Nicole looked at him, but said nothing. She wasn't sure if she was ready for any more surprises, at this point.

"Since it will be a fairly formal evening," Allen continued, "and you will be a hostess, I'd like for you to look especially smashing. I know that you are not long out of art college, and that we don't offer some of the salary and fringe benefits that we'd like to at the Galley, but in the way of compensation for the extra hours of work and effort that this project is sure to cost you, I've set up an account for you at Milady's Evening Apparel. Please go down and select a nice gown appropriate for a summer party at a beautiful estate, courtesy of The Pelican Gallery."

"Oh, I couldn't accept such a gift," murmured Nicole.

"It's not a gift. As I've already explained, it's a form of compensation in lieu of overtime pay."

"Thank you," replied Nicole.

"Well, I'm off to the airport," said Allen. "I'd ask you to drive me, but I know how much you have to do around here." He winked, and Nicole smiled.

"You are so beautiful," Allen said, taking her in his arms and kissing her. "I'll miss you while I'm away, you can be sure of that. I see you as a big part of the future of the gallery."

"I'm glad you have such confidence in me," Nicole murmured.

"It'll go fine," Allen assured her. "When in doubt, think like an artist, but keep an eye on the figures. I'll call often."

He kissed her again, and then he was gone, with a wave of his hand and a wink.

Nicole turned back to her desk. She st down and touched her cheek and her lips where Allen had kissed her. Allen was such a good friend, and he certainly would be considered by many young women to be a "good catch". Millie giggled at his jokes and often confided in Nicole that she hoped that, someday, she could find a husband like Mr. Davies. Between Marta and Allen there appeared to be a depth of understanding that surpassed even friendship, but at no time had Nicole sensed anything even remotely romantic between them. As far as Nicole knew, Allen was a very eligible bachelor. It was beginning to trouble her that she was having difficulty casting him in the role of her sweetheart. They had so much in common in their work and their their interest in art.

His kisses and hugs didn't disturb her or offend her. The were warm and nonthreatening. But neither did they move her deeply, as had the kisses of Ren Steele. Nicole sighed deeply. She had much to share with Allen, and nothing in common with Ren. She would just have to continue to push Ren out of her thoughts, for her own good and for her own peace of mind.

By the time Allen had pulled away from his parking place, Nicole had begun reviewing the notes she had taken, and was studying the menus provided by the caterer. Before she could do much else, she decided, she would have to drive out to the Mer d'Azur to actually look at the facility. She functioned best in a visual mode, and knew that she needed to have clear images of the villa's rooms and facilities to do her best work.

After having made telephone arrangements announcing the purpose of her visit, Nicole got into her car and drove west to the coastline. The Mer d'Azure was situated on several acres of land. Nicole turned onto a long sweeping driveway lined on both sides by rows of meticulously groomed palm trees. She passed through an open, wrought iron gate that looked to be a good twelve feet high, and just around a curve of the drive, she caught sight of the villa itself.

It was of a Mediterranean design popular among wealthy Florida landowners on both coasts around the turn of the twentieth century. It stood three floors high, was roofed in rusty-red barrel tiles, and the textured exterior stucco was creamy white. The tall windows on all three floors were paned with multiple squares of glass framed in black iron-work.

Nicole parked her car in the visitors' area, and walked up the wide front steps and through the massive, double-hung oak doors of the main entrance.

To the right were some offices, a coatroom and visitors' bathrooms. Nicole was greeted by a young man, who said in a graceful Cuban accent,"Welcome to the Mer d'Azure. How may I be of assistance?"

"I'm here to see Maria Sant'angelo. I'm Nicole Carpenter."

"Just a moment, please." he said, and disappeared. He emerged a short time later from one of the offices, preceded by a young woman of less than thirty. "Welcome, Miss Carpenter," she said, extending her hand. "I'm Maria."

Nicole explained her desire to personally see the site of the Pelican's reception and party, and her need for some advice and assistance in make the arrangements.

"Of course," responded Maria. "I have been speaking with Miss Marta Andress and with Mr. Davies, and I'm sure you'll like what you see. Come, let me show you through the Mer d'Azure."

Nicole followed Maria into the main reception room of the villa, and caught her breath. The space was perfect for a large, elegant evening party, ball, or wedding reception. The tile of the entry way gave way to a broad expanse of polished wood floors. The ceiling rose two full floors, and at the second level, a balcony overlooked the room. Three huge crystal chandeliers were suspended from the ceiling, and hundreds of pieces of polished glass glittered in the natural light from the windows.

"They're quite beautiful when they're lit at night," Maria commented.

She escorted Nicole through a carpeted dining area, and out through one of several sets of french doors onto a large, L-shaped terrace paved in irregularly cut slabs of stone. From the terrace, a lush, green lawn extended to the shoreline. The blue-green Gulf of Mexico met the horizon to the west.

"What a perfectly beautiful setting," breathed Nicole.

"Yes," said Maria, "but I think it's even more beautiful at might. For your party, the terrace will be strung with lights, and throughout the grounds, we have the landscaping lit from both the trees and from below, in the shrubbery. When the moonlight strikes the Gulf waters, its quite magical, really. Satisfactory?" she asked.

Nicole nodded.

"Good, let' go in then, and take care of the rest of the arrangements."

The remainder of the day, back at the Pelican, went smoothly. When Millie left at closing time, Nicole was satisfied that everything was proceeding well enough for her to take some time for herself to think about Allen's offer and suggestion that she set up a studio space for herself in the storage area.

Nicole locked the front entry, armed the security system, and closed her office door. She then made her way through the display rooms of the gallery to the storage areas.

The room that Allen had offered to Nicole for use as a studio had definite possibilities. Th concrete floor would need to be covered with drop cloths, and some of the boxes and supplies would need to be rearranged, but there was plenty of natural light from the skylights, and there was enough storage space for her art supplies.

Nicole was about to leave for the evening through the back loading entrance when she heard the telephone. She picked up the extension, and was greeted by Allen's voice.

"How was your afternoon, luv?"

"Great," said Nicole. "I went to the Mer d' Azure—it's gorgeous. I was just getting ready to leave to go shopping for my dress."

"Super," said Allen.

"How are things going where you are?"

"Well," replied Allen, "it's hard to say at this point." He didn't give any more information. "Is Marta still around?"

"No, I don't think so. Her office door is closed, but I don't think she's here."

"I'll reach her at home tonight, then. You take good care of yourself, luv, and I'll be thinking of you."

"Good night, Allen." Nicole hung up the telephone and left the gallery.

The next several days were so busy they seemed to spin by. Nicole was so tired in the evenings that she fell into deep, dreamless sleep and awoke to the music on her alarm clock with no sense at all of the night's passing. Working with Marta was not entirely pleasant. She was high-handed and difficult at times, snapping orders and questions at Nicole. Gradually, however, Nicole found that if she used a little well-placed flattery, and held her ground on the matters and details that she had strong opinions about, she and Marta could, and did, come to agreement.

One afternoon, Millie put through a call to Nicole as she was sitting in Marta's office finalizing the order for the floral arrangements. Marta handed the telephone to Nicole irritably. "Make it short, will you?"

She put out her cigarette and left the room.

"Hi," Aunt Jane," Nicole said, ignoring Marta's stagy exit. She excitedly filled Aunt Jane in on the details of the upcoming party.

"Sounds elegant," responded Aunt Jane. "Will you be able to come back to the Cypress for another visit when it's over?"

"I suppose so," Nicole said vaguely.

"Where's Allen while all this is going on?" questioned her aunt.

"He's been out of town. I don't think he'll be back until just before the party. He's had to go to several cities to take care of some business."

"Really," said Jane. "Must be important if he had to leave you to arrange the party."

"I suppose so," repeated Nicole. "I hadn't really thought that much about it."

"M-mm," responded her aunt. Nicole had the impression that something was troubling Aunt Jane.

"Allen's all right, I'm sure," said Nicole. "He calls pretty often to see how things are going."

"That's good" said Aunt Jane, "but you're the one I'm concerned about. I don't like to think of you working so hard."

Nicole laughed merrily. "It must run in the family, I guess."

She paused, and then went on. "Allen seems to have it in mind that he's grooming me for a more important role with the business."

"How do you feel about it?" asked Aunt Jane.

"Good. I like the work, and I like Naples." She hesitated, and then decided to confided in her aunt. "I also think that Allen may be interested in me romantically."

Aunt Jane did not seem surprised. "And how about you? Are you becoming interested in him, too?"

"I don't know," said Nicole slowly. "It's kind of confusing, actually. I don't know quite how I feel."

"Well, take your time. You've been through a lot of changes and some difficult times in just a short while. Why don't I invite you back out to the Cypress after that party? Allen certainly owes you some time off. Take some time for yourself to think about what you really want for your life."

Marta re-entered her office, her heels clicking on the marble floor.

"Thank you, Aunt Jane," Nicole ended. "I'll call you about coming out some time after the party."

"Going back out into the muck, are we?" Marta said airily.

Nicole didn't respond to Marta's provocation. What she did with her personal time was none of Marta's business.

"Well, then, let's get on with it," Marta said. "We have some very important guests who will be attending, and I want everything to be perfect."

The day of the party dawned warm and clear. Nicole had her coffee on her patio, and then went inside to lay out her clothes and jewelry for the evening. She dressed for work, and then drove out to the Mer d'Azure, where she was to meet Marta to help supervise the final arrangements.

When she arrived, she found Marta directing the hanging of some of the art she had brought out from the

Pelican. Marta was dressed in a soft knit amethyst dress that floated just above her knees. She looked comfortably in charge. He long auburn hair shone with gold in the light slanting through the windows of the estate, and she appeared to be full of energy and good spirits.

"Shall we hang these two here, where they'll be seen first thing when people arrive?" Marta asked Nicole.

Nicole regarded the two oil paintings. They were both interpretations of a lily pond, and both were of excellent quality. One was done more representationally, in shades of blue and green with pink and white blooms. In the other, more impressionistic painting, the water was splashed with golden light, and lily flowers were rose-colored.

Nicole looked up. The only lighting in the immediate area was from recessed bulbs in the ceiling, and they didn't appear to be of very high wattage. Nicole noticed there was no wall outlet nearby, either.

"We could," she said slowly. "They'll fill the space nicely, and they're fine oils we'd want everyone to notice. But, the light here this evening won't show them off to any advantage unless we get some battery-powered lights for just over the frames, but those could distort the textures of the surfaces."

Marta looked at her, and nodded. "You're right, I think," She said grudgingly. "Where, then?"

Nicole looked around the large reception hall. "How about over there, on the wall just as people come through to the serving area? There's some track lighting that could probably be adjusted to highlight them well."

"That would do," Marta agreed. She walked to the center of the large reception room. "I thought the harpist could set up here. She said she's performed in this venue for other events, and likes the acoustics. She's asked for a small table near by with a pitcher of water. I've already told Maria what she wants."

By noon, with the help of the villa's staff, the art had been hung, and the arrangements completed. The florist had delivered a selection of large, potted palms and ficus trees, which the Pelican Gallery had leased for the evening. Nicole had decided that the cut flowers for the tables and buffet would be primarily bird-of paradise. The villa's staff had been able to order both blue and golden table coverings, to complement the floral arrangements.

"Well, that's it then," said Marta in her clipped way. "I'll run through the guest list with you—and then, we'll meet back here at six this evening. I'm not quite sure what time Allen is scheduled to get in, but I'm not going to worry about it. He knows his way out here."

Nicole looked at Marta in sudden surprise.

"What, now?" asked Marta, her characteristic irritation surfacing.

"Nothing of importance," Nicole replied, lowering her eyes. There was something about the way Marta pronounced some of her words that occasionally sounded British. She supposed that working with Allen had had its effect on her speech patterns. Nicole sometimes found that she, too, had picked up a phrase from him or a bit of pronunciation.

"Well, then," continued Marta, "let's go through this guest list and be done with it."

Marta handed Nicole a copy, which she began to scan for familiar names. She recognized members of the Naples and Collier County arts councils, some artists, and some of the Pelican's customers with whom she had had contact.

"The names that are checked have confirmed their attendance with Millie. The names that have asterisks I want you to pay special heed to, as they are people of prime importance to us."

As Nicole continued to scan the alphabetized guest list, she froze. "Mr. Ren Steele," she said in a whisper. How had he managed to get himself on the guest list for this event, Nicole wondered, her fury mounting. Was there no place she could escape from him?

"Ah, yes, Mr. Steele," purred Marta. "He's not of much importance to the Naples art world at this time, although it is said that he has an appreciation for beauty and the means to finance his tastes. Rather, he will be my escort for the evening."

Nicole stared at Marta, unable to utter a single word. She was swept with wave after wave of powerful, confusing emotions: shock, anger, betrayal, outrage, confusion, and—most humiliating of all—a painful jealousy. Initially, she had felt the blood drain from her face, but now, her skin felt as if it was burning. There could be no way she would be able to endure the evening. She would have to find a means of escape.

By the time Nicole had arrived back at the gallery, she had calmed herself considerably. A cool, angry resolve had replaced the tumultuous flood of emotion that had been released at Marta's news that Ren Steele would be her date for the party. Why should she care who Ren Steele escorted, or of what his private life consisted? She had worked very hard on the party, and she was determined that it would be a success. She would be polite to Ren, but she would avoid him as much as possible. She would have plenty to busy herself with, and many guests to attend to, so it should be relatively easy to focus on other matters. As far as Marta and Ren, it simply confirmed her original assessment that Ren was a playboy not to be taken seriously. It simple did not matter, Nicole told herself firmly, how Ren and Marta had come to know each other well enough so that he would be attending the party with her.

Allen pulled in to his parking space at about 4:30, just as Nicole was getting ready to leave the gallery to go home and get dressed for the evening. He looked tired and careworn, Nicole noticed. She felt sorry for him, imagining the stress and difficulty of working out of town most of the week and then having to return to host the Pelican's reception.

He put on a cheerful face when he saw Nicole, and listened attentively as she described the arrangements recently completed at the Mer d'Azur.

"We make a good team, don't you think?" he asked. Nicole nodded. "Perhaps we should consider a more permanent arrangement."

Nicole shrugged diffidently, not wanting to pursue the subject with Allen just before the party.

"I'm going home to get dressed," Nicole said.

"I'll come by for you in about an hour, then," said Allen.

Chapter 9

A rosy-orange sun was just beginning its descent toward the waters of the Gulf of Mexico when Allen and Nicole arrived at the Mer d'Azure. Allen had rented a limousine for the evening, and as the chauffeur helped her out of the back of the long, white car, Nicole admired the estate's grounds. The trees and some of the larger azaleas were lit with thousands of tiny white lights, outdoor Christmas tree lights Nicole imagined, giving the beautifully landscaped setting a festive quality.

A door man greeted them politely, and they were met by Maria and a member of her staff. The first guests weren't due for another fifteen minutes, or so.

"I'm going to see to how the art is hung, and take a look at the table set ups." Allen said, rather anxiously. Nicole, who had been so directly involved in arranging the event, was less concerned. She had developed a confidence in the Mer d'Azure's staff, and felt certain all was well.

""You go ahead," she said. "I think I'll stay here in the main hall and wait for people to arrive."

"Good idea," replied Allen. "I'll be just over there," he said, indicating the dining room and the main display area of the Pelican's art. "I like the choice of paintings in the foyer, by the way."

Nicole smiled, and followed Allen with her eyes as he made his way across the reception hall to the dining area. His steps were quick, and he seemed to take in everything with short glances.

The harpist had set up and was ready to play on schedule. She wore a floor-length black dress with white accents, and her black hair was piled on top her head and secured with whit gardenia blossoms. She seated herself at her instrument, and as her fingers began to caress and explore the strings, the lovely strains of a piece Nicole did not recognize filled the hall. The acoustics of the nearly empty space would change as it filled with people, Nicole understood, but for the present, she rather enjoyed the way the music seemed to glide over the hard, smooth surfaces of the room and rise toward the high ceiling above.

Nicole walked around, admiring the florist's work. He had taken Nicole's recommendations about color, and her desire for many large foliage plants and trees, and had transformed and softened the spaces with tall ficus tress, potted palms, and groupings of flowering azaleas. Some of the larger trees were strung with tiny white lights, illuminating the spaces around them softly. All-in-all, Nicole decided, the stage had been set for a beautiful evening. But, one that will test my every reserve of control and self-discipline, she thought sadly.

The first guests began to arrive, and Nicole noted with pleasure their expectant air and their admiring glances around the softly lit, graciously decorated hall. She walked up t an elderly man accompanied by tow women in their fifties—his daughters perhaps—and greeted them.

"I'm Nicole Carpenter, from the Pelican Gallery. Welcome. Would you care for something to drink?'

She glanced at a waiter, who caught her eye and brought a tray of filled champagne glasses and canapes.

"Arlen Sykes," said the man, extending his hand to Nicole. "This is Marla Hightower and Rose Mercks. Notice any family resemblances?"

Nicole smiled. Marla Hightower was on the Collier County Council for the Arts, and Arlen Sykes was a developer and financier for Naples' new and strikingly beautiful arts complex, which featured a museum and concert hall. They lived in the Port Royal area and were considered "old money" by Collier County standards.

"No champagne for me," said Mr. Sykes, "doctor's orders. He wants to keep me alive as long as possible, or at least until he pays off his Jaguar and his new house in Venetian Beach. Ginger ale, please."

Within just a few minutes, the hall had begun to fill with the sounds of good-natured conversation as more guests arrived and greeted each other. Nicole looked around anxiously for Allen. She had done her best to learn a little bit about everyone on the guest list, but she was getting concerned that she might forget some names and do a poor job with introductions. Fortunately, in a town as small as Naples, most people at the party could be expected to have at least a passing acquaintance with one another, and many saw each other regularly in the course of business, charity functions, and arts-related activities.

"Looks like it'll be a nice evening with a good turn out," commented Mr. Sykes.

"We hope so," said Nicole.

"It's nice to come to one of these large functions without being asked to contribute something to some charity or the other," he winked.

"Our way of introducing the gallery to people who don't know us well and saying thank you to those who do," Nicole said with a smile.

"Do you paint?" he asked.

"Not as much as I'd like. I'll be doing more over the summer," Nicole replied.

"While a lot of us will be going up north," he nodded.

"Do you have a summer home somewhere?" Nicole asked politely.

"Not any more, not really." Mr. Sykes replied. "We still have a house on Nantucket," he said, nodding in the direction of his daughters, "but since their mother died, we haven't gone much. In fact, I've decided to rent it out for the whole season."

Nicole nodded sympathetically. Out of the corner of her eye, she saw Allen making his rounds among the guests, greeting them by name with his easy, charming smile. He shook hands with the men, and dropped friendly compliments on the older women concerning their tastes in fashion and self-adornment.

Nicole turned away from Mr. Sykes when he seemed ready to engage in conversation with a local banker, and began to circulate among the guests. The conversation level was growing louder as more people came in, and the harpist was playing a piece at a moderate tempo in a major key. The music wafted above the level of the conversations at times, filling the room with good cheer.

A group of people had gathered by one of the larger floral displays, and Nicole joined them.

"I think this drought has brought out the chinch bugs," a woman was saying. Nicole recognized her as a real estate broker and a collector of fine water colors. "The watering restrictions are doing a number on the lawns, making them stressed and vulnerable. Makes it harder for properties to show well."

"Well, I don't care if the whole lawn dries up," said a man in a yellow sports jacket and a flowered tie. "We'll be leaving for Hyannis next week."

"You'll care when we have to re-sod the whole thing in the fall," snapped his wife.

"I'll worry about that when we get back," he retorted good-naturedly. "All I can think about now is getting the sail boat out onto Nantucket Sound.

He wife snorted "He lives for that boat. I won't see him on any day that the weather's fit for sailing."

"Isn't there quite a bit of fog up that way?" someone asked.

"Mainly in the early summer. June. Depends on the year."

"Well, we're staying here all summer," remarked a woman in a long, dark blue sequined gown. "We got sick of making the trek back and forth to Maine every year."

"I don't like to stay here through hurricane season," commented another.

"We haven't had one in a while," added a man. "We could be due for one this year."

"Well, at least a hurricane would put an end to the drought," someone joked.

"It could take at least a Category 3 to put an end to the Marlins' batting slump."

As the conversation turned to baseball and soccer, Nicole made her way to the buffet, which had just been brought out by the catering staff. She caught sight of herself in a long mirror, and brushed a tendril of dark hair from her forehead.

For this special evening, Nicole had chosen to dress in black. She wore a sleeveless party dress with a short, layered skirt. The bodice of the dress and the filmy outer layer of the skirt were scattered with silvery sparkles. She wore silky black hosiery, high-heeled strappy sandals with silver buckles, and her mother's diamond earrings. Her long hair was pulled away from her face in to a french braid, into which she had woven strands of black sequins sewn onto black satin ribbons. She smiled at herself to soften her slightly worried expression.

"That's better," said Allen, approaching her in the mirror from behind. "You have such a beautiful smile, you know.'

"I'm okay," smiled Nicole. "Still a little nervous."

"What's to be nervous about?" asked Allen. Things seem to be going swimmingly."

Nicole turned and surveyed the room. People indeed seemed to be enjoying themselves.

"Who are those people over there?" asked Nicole, indicating a group standing near the buffet table. "The man in the blue suit looks familiar somehow, but I can't place him."

"Ah," replied Allen, "I shouldn't wonder that he looks familiar. You've seen his face enough times."

Nicole looked puzzled.

Cyrus B. Teague. He's running for Collier County Sheriff in the next election. Posters are up all around. His family has been in the county forever."

Nicole nodded. "That explains it. But, I don't recall his name on the guest list.

Allen shrugged. "Probably came along with the Dowds or the Andersons," he replied, indicating the group with which Mr. Teague was conversing. "They're all in development, and aside from Mrs. Dowd and Mrs. Anderson fancying themselves to be collectors of fine art, they're no doubt potential campaign contributors. Or, our Mr. Teague may have hopes in that direction."

"What kind of art do they like?" asked Nicole. "I don't think I've ever seen either Mrs. Dowd or Mrs. Anderson in the gallery.

"Antiquities, from what I hear. Let's mingle, shall we?" Allen steered Nicole toward the buffet table. "Have I told you how lovely you look this evening?"

"Once or twice," Nicole said with a smile.

"I hope you won't become bored any time soon with my admiration of your beauty. It's a weakness I have, you see."

"A weakness?" Nicole smiled, raising her eyebrows in mock surprise. "I didn't know you had any."

"I have a few, I'm afraid. But not too many, I hope, for you to rule me out as a suitable partner some day." Allen was still smiling, but his eyes wee tender and serious-looking.

Nicole looked at Allen. Behind him, the party swirled, now in full swing. The women in their colorful dresses and sparkling jewels and the men in their dark or white jackets created with their motion a kaleidoscope of changing patterns.

Allen turned to speak with a group of well-dressed women who had arrived together, and Nicole stepped away, thinking of taking a moment to get a breath of fresh air. As she headed toward the front of the hall, she noticed three men, including Mr. Teague, staring in the direction of the main entrance.

Nicole stopped in her tracks and caught her breath. Ren Steele had crossed the threshold, a look of amusement on his tanned, attractive features. He was wearing a classic tuxedo that fit him to perfection. His hair was recently barbered. He seemed entirely comfortable in his attire, as if he attended events in evening dress so frequently that the clothes were as natural-feeling to him as the jeans and boots he wore in the Everglades. Nicole stared, taking in every detail of his graceful, easy entrance. She felt surprisingly calm at finally seeing him, almost as if she were watching a Cary Grant movie rather than seeing Ren Steele in real life.

Time seemed to have slowed, but it couldn't have been more that a few moments before her attention was diverted to the woman clinging to Ren's arm. Nicole felt a hot flush of confusion. Marta Andress was wearing an extremely slinky emerald green designer gown cut daringly low, exposing the tops of her bosom. Her auburn hair was curled in ringlets and pulled up to spill out in seductive disarray from a green feathered headpiece. She was holding on to Ren possessively, and when she caught

Nicole looking at her, she flashed a dazzling, malicious grin.

Nicole's breath finally seemed to return when Allen signaled his presence at her side by lightly touching the back of her arm. Ren and Marta walked past them into the crowd with polite nods to various guests.

"What is she up to, now?" Allen asked, as if he were speaking to himself. "Oh, well," he shrugged, "that's Marta for you. Never one to miss the main chance. She could spot a shilling in a slag-heap at fifty paces."

Nicole barely heard him. Her initial composure had begun to give way to a restless, urgent need to get moving. She had believed she had prepared herself for the evening ahead, but, confronted with the reality of seeing Ren and the very worldly, seductive Marta together, she was shaken and disturbed.

Ren looked exceedingly handsome, even more so than she had remembered. His male presence was powerful and almost wild-seeming in the room full of wealthy, well-connected men. His clothes were no more well-tailored than those of the bankers and executives and the comfortably retired men who were also at the party, but he wore the clothes over a tight, muscled physique and moved with an athlete's unconscious grace and confidence.

He was staying close to Marta, his hand at the small of her back. Marta appeared lit from within, her features softened attractively as she looked up at him. Nicole turned away, lost and desolate, completely unaware of Allen's concerned look and tight smile.

Nicole found herself staring at a floral display of potted palms and ficus. The lush, tropical greenery reminded her of the woodlands around the Cypress Retreat. She was unaccountably taken back to the night she had stepped outside for a breath of air onto the patio near her room at her aunt's guest lodge. There had been the rustle of branches, and then Ren had appeared and had taken her in is arms for the first time and she had known the disturbing, sweet power of his kisses.

She had struggled against surrendering to her feelings that night, and she had resisted being swept along by the currents of desire and need that Ren aroused in her so easily each time he had taken her in his arms, and now he was with another woman, a beautiful woman, and one who might not find the temptation of Ren's sensuous mouth on hers something to resist at all.

Jealousy and despair pelted Nicole like a cold rain. Had she made herself so stubborn and angry at Ren that he had no choice but to turn to warmer, more receptive arms?

No, she reminded herself, it might have been stubborn, but it was smart, and safe, and self-protective to resist a man who had shown himself clearly to be so shallow and vacillating in feeling that he went from one woman to another with no backward look. Some men were like that, Nicole knew, and they brought heartbreak and disappointment to the women who fell fatally under their spell.

Nicole did not want the pain of a doomed relationship with a man who shared his kisses casually. She had been raised by loving and devoted parents, and if she married, it would be to a solid and reliable man who cared more for her feelings and less for his own careless pleasure-taking.

She turned to Allen, as if she were seeing him for the first time.

"Sorry," she said with a calm smile. "I got lost there for a spell. Shall we go have some of the buffet?"

Allen nodded.

They made their way to the serving line. Nicole held Allen's arm. She straightened her shoulders, and wiped away a film of moisture from her forehead with the back of her hand.

"It's a warm night, isn't it?" a man in front of them asked, noticing her gesture.

"It is," agreed Nicole. "We have some cold dishes to choose from," she pointed out, once more the Gallery's hostess. "There's iced tea and other cold drinks to be had, too."

"Thank you," the man said. "It's good to drink plenty of liquids, or so my doctor tells me."

Nicole nodded, and smiled at Allen, behind her. Allen winked back.

"Shall we sit over there?" he asked, indicating a table outside on the terrace. "We could chat up the Browns and Mrs. Renquist. Good conversationalists. Mrs. Renquist has some perfectly astute observations on Naples high society, if you don't mind the risk of being future fodder for her next dinner party."

Nicole laughed. "I'm game."

After dinner, Allen excused himself, and Nicole got up from her seat to join the Renquists for a stroll around the terrace. Mr. Renquist lit a sweet-smelling cigar. Mrs. Renquist made a face and confided in Nicole her dislike of the cigars.

"He lives for the day when Cuban cigars will be freely available in Florida. Whenever we go down to the Caymans, his first stop is the duty-free smoke shops."

"And yours is the jewelry stores," Mr. Renquist returned good naturedly.

"At least I can legally bring the jewelry back into the country," she said levelly. "I'm in horror," she said, turning to Nicole, "of the day that customs searches his bags and finds his little stash of Havana contraband."

"I always tell her not to worry, that United States Customs has more important things to do than bother an old man about a couple of Cuban cigars."

"Well, possibly so," Mrs. Renquist agreed, "but I still insist that we pack separate bags and fill out separate declaration forms. I'll be darned if I'm going to be fined or sent to jail over his cigars."

"Could that really happen?" asked Nicole.

Mrs. Renquist shrugged. "I don't like to take any chances."

"Sarah likes to worry needlessly", Mr. Renquist explained to Nicole.

"Well, you'd better hope it's needless worry, "Mrs. Renquist snapped, ending the discussion.

Nicole turned away, slightly uncomfortable at the tension between the Renquists. She didn't know either one of them well enough to referee a marital disagreement.

"Good evening, Nicole," said Ren Steele, at that moment stepping out onto the terrace. He was alone.

"Good evening, Mr. Steele," Nicole replied politely, but with a chill in her voice.

"Good evening" he said, nodding to the Renquists. They nodded back, and, determining that their presence might constitute a breach of privacy, strolled away to the end of the terrace.

"Would you care to go for a walk?" Ren asked Nicole after the Renquists were out of hearing range.

"No, thank you," Nicole declined. "I was just getting ready to go back inside."

"Is that so?" asked Ren, with a devilish grin. "You look to me like you just decided that within the past fifteen seconds."

"There are guests to attend to," Nicole said stiffly.

"I'm a guest," Ren pointed out. "I need attending to."

"Perhaps Marta will be able to help you. That's her department, isn't it?" retorted Nicole icily. She turned way from him and walked to the edge of the terrace.

The moon had risen, and, in its path, had lit up a great swath of the still waters of the Gulf of Mexico. The slight, rolling swells of the incoming tide sparkled and danced in its light. The air was still and warm. The sky was soft and clear. The evening star hung low on the horizon, and other stars, fainter, were beginning to show themselves as the evening deepened. A few bands of high clouds were illuminated against the dark sky by the moonlight.

"A perfectly romantic evening, is it not?" asked Ren from behind her.

Nicole turned, ready to lambaste him for his arrogance and his presumptuousness in following her when she so clearly wanted nothing to do with him. She found, however, that he was addressing himself to two middle-aged women standing beside him, admiring the view from the terrace.

Oh, yes, it certainly is," said one of them.

"A beautiful evening" agreed the other.

Nicole recognized them as artists whose work was marketed primarily through the Pelican Gallery. The one, Mrs. Hopkins, painted beach scapes which sold reliably, and the other, Alice Simpson, worked mainly in pastels.

Millie had confided in Nicole that they shared a studio, and lived together on Marco Island.

"How are you enjoying the party?" Nicole asked, careful not to look at Ren.

"Oh, very much," replied Mrs. Simpson.

"Oh, yes, very nice," agreed Mrs. Hopkins. "We don't get out very much in the evening, so this is quite a treat."

Ren hovered nearby, Nicole noticed, not intruding in the conversation, but not making any effort to distance himself, either. Music from the speakers mounted on the stucco walls of the building began to drift into the night, a soft, romantic Cole Porter ballad. The melody floated beguilingly in the soft, warm air. The terrace was beginning to fill with guests, now that dinner was over.

"Would you care to dance, Miss Carpenter?" Ren asked politely, with a charming smile cast at the ladies. They giggled like schoolgirls, anticipating Nicole's response.

Nicole felt trapped. Certainly, she was free to decline. She looked at Mrs. Simpson and Mrs. Hopkins. Their faces were wistful with memories of long-ago dances.

"Oh, please do, Miss Carpenter," Mrs. Simpson urged. "It's much too beautiful a night to say 'no'. Do you remember, Mildred, how you danced to this tune in Chicago, at the Starlight Room, the night Henry proposed to you? I was with that Ken Mitchell, remember?"

Mrs. Hopkins nodded, looking expectantly at Nicole.

Nicole sighed, feeling defeated. She looked up at Ren with a small nod, and he stepped forward, taking her gently and respectfully in his arms. Nicole placed her arm over his, and rested her hand lightly on his shoulder. Ren took her right hand and held it to his chest, guiding he smoothly and expertly to the slow, dreamy sway of he music. Nicole closed her eyes, waiting for the tune to end so she could make her escape, having played her part for the guests.

Ren pulled her closer, and Nicole inhaled his familiar, masculine scent, a clean blend of soap and a subtle aftershave. They moved together to the sensual rhythms of the music, Nicole perfectly anticipating his lead.

"We dance well together, Nicole," he murmured.

Nicole stiffened. He had taken advantage of the situation, but the song would end soon. She turned her head away from him. His lips brushed her hair, and she felt his warm breath. Her scalp tingled, and she tossed her head, shaking off the tantalizing sensual spell this man was beginning to draw around her. He came here with Marta, Nicole reminded herself, and he will be going home with Marta.

"Ah, there you are, Nicole," said Allen, approaching them as the song ended. "I'd wondered what had become of you."

The music had stopped, but Ren did not immediately release Nicole from his arms. The terrace was emptying, as the guests began to say their goodbyes. Nicole saw Marta several paces away, holding her green evening bag and looking pointedly in their direction. Apparently, she could not wait to claim Ren once their dance ended, when she would have him for the remainder of the evening and, perhaps, for the night.

The image of Marta in Ren's arms grew vividly in Nicole's imagination. He would hold her as he kissed her, and Marta would feel his hard, warm, muscled body and his hot breath in her auburn hair. Perhaps she would slowly remove that feathered hat and unpin her long hair for Ren. Nicole squeezed ere eyes shut to force away thoughts of their love-making.

She simply could not bear the torment of the moment. The tension of the day, coupled with Nicole's exhaustion from her long hours of work for the party, had crescendoed, and finally, she had no reserve of emotional energy.

Impulsively, she freed herself from Ren's casual embrace, and turned to Allen.

"I've been thinking abut your proposal," she said to him. "I think you're right. We would make good partnership."

Nicole felt a moment of triumph having made her small declaration of freedom from Ren's disturbing hold on her emotional life. She cast a sidelong look at him, as he stood motionless beside her. His face had become an unreadable mask, except for his blue eyes, which were cold, cold as steel. Nicole smiled at the pun she had made on his name, and Ren shot her an icy look that devastated her. He held out his elbow to Marta, and said to her gently, "Shall we, my dear?". Marta practically leaped at the invitation, and without a backward look, Ren strode off into the night, Marta swaying beside him in her long dress and high heels.

Numbly, Nicole watched them leave. What had come over her? In just the space of a few minutes, she had gone from feeling angry at Ren for manipulating her by asking her to dance in a social situation where she found it too awkward to decline, to beginning to fall fatally under his spell again as she swayed with him to the music under the starlight, to being pierced by sharp, unexpected jealousy at the image of Ren and Marta intimately alone together. Then, from nowhere, she had heard herself impulsively tell Allen that she might marry him—had he even actually, specifically asked her?--and foolishly enjoyed, for a few seconds, Ren's reaction to her spontaneous and hurtful eruption. Now, she was standing with Allen at her side, feeling as alone as she ever had before in her life. She looked at Allen's hopeful face, and felt the sharp sting of tears in her eyes.

Her feelings for Allen had confused her almost as much as her feelings for Ren had. She had been terribly vulnerable in her grief at the sudden deaths of her parents when she had first come to work at the Pelican Galley, and, with the pain of that loss still fresh, she had welcomed Allen's friendship and tutelage on the job. Gradually, their work and their social life had begun to merge. It had seemed entirely natural to accept Allen's small gestures of caring and consideration, and she had been flattered by his compliments and by his encouragement of her painting and her career development. It had been easy to admire Allen, with his casual social grace and his experience and expertise in the world of art she had been so eager for so long to join. Was it possible without quite realizing how it had happened that she had overlooked Allen's feelings and had, perhaps, led him to hope that she was developing a romantic interest in him? In truth, she had never felt more for him than friendship, and here he was, standing at her side, looking at her with expectation and anticipation.

"Did I hear what I thought I just did?" he asked softly. "Have you, in fact, my dear, been thinking about us as a partnership? If so, I apologize for not having been more romantic and ardent in my pursuit of your hand. Despite what you might think," he went on, "I'm not so confident in matters of the heart, and I haven't felt, if you'll forgive me or saying so, much interest on your part. You're so young..."

His voice trailed off. Nicole looked at him, feeling deeply his vulnerability in this moment. Her sensitivity to him seemed to have been given depth and resonance by her own acute suffering. Allen's eyes were so questioning, and she could feel his emotions as if they were her own. He stood before her, hoping and yet not daring to hope too much.

"But, if you are serious," he continued, taking her gently and tentatively in his arms, "I would be yours, forever."

Nicole smiled through a glaze of tears. Tonight, she had grown up, and knew the pain of being an adult woman who had just let the only man who had ever fully aroused her passion and need walk out the door with another woman.

How much time had passed since Ren and Marta had left the Mer d'Azur? All the guests were gone, and the staff was cleaning up the terrace, respectfully giving

Nicole and Allen their privacy. Certainly enough time for Ren and Marta to be locked in an embrace at some romantic, moonlight-strewn beach.

It would serve me right, Nicole thought bitterly as she left the estate with Allen. The party had been a wonderful success, a triumph of her organizational skills and her artistic taste, but her personal life was a disaster. On a warm, tropical evening by the Gulf of Mexico, she had lost forever the man she loved to another woman's more willing arms because she had realized, too late, the significance of the powerful response he had never failed to arouse in her. And, now, she had another man's heart in her hand.

She barely listened as Allen drove her home, talking about the possibilities that life together would hold for the two of them. Finally, she turned to him as tenderly as possible.

"I hope you'll understand, Allen, but tonight is really not a good time for us to be talking about a future for us together, I'm simply too exhausted by the stress of the party. I need some time to unwind."

"Of course, my darling," said Allen, nodding sagely. "But you can understand how eager I am. Might we have dinner together tomorrow? Would seven o'clock be convenient?"

Nicole nodded. Tomorrow was Saturday. She could sleep late. She prayed her dreams wouldn't torment her.

CHAPTER 10

Nicole stood before her mirrored closet door and stared at her reflection. She held up a rose-colored sleeveless dress. The color made her look sallow, and seemed to bring out the dark circles under her eyes. She sighed, and tossed the dress on to the bed, on top of blue one she had already rejected. Allen would be leaving his house soon to pick her up for their dinner date and she wouldn't be dressed by the time he arrived if she didn't decide on something from her wardrobe soon.

After a fretful, restless night of half-sleep, Nicole had spent most of the day in a mental fog. She would be hard-pressed, she reflected, to account for how she had passed the hours after her morning coffee.

She was not anticipating the evening ahead with any pleasure. Allen's expectations for their dinner date were high, Nicole knew, but she herself felt flat and emotionally spent.

She wondered how she would respond if Allen formally proposed to her. She was no farther along in figuring out what to do than she had been last night when she had realized his intentions and had deferred any discussion until tonight. Nicole sighed deeply and pressed the palms of her hands to her forehead. Perhaps she should do the practical thing and accept his proposal, if he asked her to marry him. There were many worse ways to spend a lifetime than with a thoughtful, attractive man who adored her. Perhaps, over time, their friendship and shared interests would prove to be as solid a base for a marriage as anyone could rightfully hope.

Nicole thought of her parents' stable and mutually-supportive relationship, and wondered how it had been at the beginning, before Nicole was born. Had there ever been the conflict and confusion and passion that had characterized her doomed and unhappy relationship with Ren? Nicole could not imagine either her mother or father at such adds and cross-purposes as she and Ren had been. Their partnership seemed to have had more similarities with her own friendly, companionable relations with Allen, at least during the years of her childhood and adolescence back to which her conscious memories extended. Of course, Nicole understood, a child's perspective of a marriage could never match that of an adult's.

Nicole had dressed, finally, and was waiting for Allen when her cell phone rang. She reached for it, expecting it to be Allen saying he was running a little late, but instead she was surprised to find that it was Aunt Jane calling her.

"Oh, hi, Aunt Jane. How are you?" Nicole asked.

"None too well, I'm sorry to say."

"Whats the matter?" Nicole asked with concern.

"Can't talk about it over the telephone." Aunt Jane's voice sounded strained and weak. Nicole felt a rush of dread fill her heart. "I need you to come out right away, as soon as you can. I absolutely must see you."

"Why, what's the matter, Aunt Jane?" Nicole asked again.

"It's urgent," said her aunt. Can you come this evening?"

"Are you all right?"

"No, I'm not all right. I simple have to see you. I'll tell you about it when you get here. You can come, can't you?"

Nicole felt cold fear spreading. Aunt Jane must be terribly ill or in some dire trouble that she couldn't share over the telephone. Nicole tried to remember if her aunt had said anything about her health or a doctor's appointment.

"I'll leave right away," Nicole said.

"I'll be waiting for you."

Nicole though she detected a rough, hoarseness in her aunt's voice that she had never heard before. She then remembered that Allen was coming to pick her up.

She scribbled a note for him, and realizing that it was almost illegible, she decided to try calling his home in case he hadn't left yet.

He answered the telephone on the sixth ring.

"I was just on my way out the door," Allen said cheerily. "Sorry I'm so late. Business calls, and all that."

"Aunt Jane's not well," Nicole said. "I'm leaving to drive out there as soon as I get off the phone. I thought I'd try calling you instead of just leaving a note. I'm glad I reached you so you didn't have to drive over here."

"I'm sorry to hear this," said Allen cautiously. "What's wrong?"

"I'm not sure. She sounds terrible, She asked me to come right away."

"It's that serious?" asked Allen.

"I'm afraid so," replied Nicole, trying not to succumb to her mounting dread. If she lost her aunt, she would be alone in the world.

Nicole drove east out of Naples, anxiously looking ahead to each set of traffic lights, trying to avoid as many red lights as possible. The sun was very low on the horizon behind her, glaring orange in her rear view mirror. Ahead, the sky had turned an ominous purple-gray. Towering black clouds looked ready to spill rain. Almost at once, a few drops began to appear on her windshield. They spread in beads horizontally, and flew off into the wind when they reached the edges of the glass.

Nicole turned on her headlights and her windshield wipers. On Route 41, a few miles outside of Naples, raindrops began pelting her car. Within moments, the sun set completely, and torrents of wind-driven rain from the east were unleashed. Nicole slowed down to thirty miles an hour. If she drove any faster, it felt like she was unsafely exceeding the reach of her headlights.

The heavy drops of rain could be seen bouncing back up from the road surface. Soon, water was pouring off both sides of the roadway into the drainage ditches which paralleled the highway. Nicole gripped the steering wheel. Her palms were moist with anxious perspiration.

High-beam headlights of an approaching truck lit up her rear view mirror. Nicole flicked up the mirror so that the blaze of light was not cast directly into her eyes. The truck was not slowing down appreciably; it mean to pass her. Nicole gripped the steering wheel firmly in anticipation of the ricocheting blast of air from the huge eighteen-wheeler as it flew past her. With what seemed like one moments, the truck's red taillights receded ahead of her. Nicole accelerated in an effort to keep the taillights in view, to use as a guide through the night.

The darkness ahead was split open by a blaze of jagged, shivering lightening, followed within two or three seconds by a loud creek of thunder crashing around the car. Nicole's night vision was briefly impaired by the lightening. She could no longer make out any trace of tail lights ahead, and slowed the car to a crawl.

Nicole was not unaccustomed to driving in South Florida thunder storms. However, it had been months sine it had rained so heavily, and Nicole could not recall a time she had driven through such a torrential downpour so far from streetlights and well-marked roadways. The gusts of wind were driving the rain onto the windshield with such force and volume of water that, even at high speed, the windshield wipers did not keep the glass clear for more than a fraction of a second at each pass of the blades.

No more traffic was behind or ahead of her car as Nicole crept along the desolate stretch of roadway, holding tightly to the steering wheel as gusts of wind of almost tropical storm force buffeted her vehicle. She prayed that no more huge trucks roared up behind her, honking and flashing their headlights to pass.

Minutes went by, and there was no appreciable slowing of the rain pouring from the dark night skies. Nicole peered over her steering wheel, looking for someplace to turn off the road and wait for the worst of the storm to pass, but this far east of Naples, the highway seemed to stretch on for miles without any intersections.

Nicole kept her eyes fixed on the road ahead, fearful of drifting off-center or getting blown by a fierce gust onto the narrow shoulder. The rain drops no longer seemed to be bouncing with such force off her windshield, but the black stretch of highway seemed to be almost alive with silvery, hopping droplets of water.

Nicole stare at the leaping bubbles lit up by her headlights. They were tiny frogs or toads, she realized, dozens and dozens of them, hopping onto the wet road from the grassy shoulders and popping up into the beams of light cast by Nicole's car.

Near the turnoff to Everglades City, the rain seemed like it was slackening. Nicole accelerated again, feeling safer with the gradual diminishing of the cloudburst. She was eager for the tension-filled drive to end, her mind once more fixed on the goal of reaching her aunt as quickly as she could.

She wondered if her aunt had seen a doctor yet, and if that doctor was well-qualified to diagnose and treat what ever was wrong. Perhaps, she would offer to bring Aunt Jane back to Naples with her, where, Nicole believed, there might be better medical care than out in the rural reaches of Collier or Hendry Counties.

Just after she crossed Highway 29 and the lights at that intersection had receded, Nicole suddenly came upon a good-sized gray animal with huge red eyes staring at her from the center of the lane. She swerved sharply to the left to avoid hitting it, and then the car was skidding and spinning on the slick road. Nicole reflexively turned the steering wheel in the opposite direction of the skid, and an instant later, she was facing down an embankment, her headlights illuminating the clear water flowing in the deep drainage canal.

Calmly and quickly she put on her parking brake and carefully opened the driver's side door. She undid her seat belt clasp with a quick motion, and got out of the car, slipping and sliding on the wet grass on the slope of the embankment. Only when she was standing at the side of the road, did she feel the surge of adrenaline that turned her legs to rubber. She sat down at the edge of the pavement, and began to cry. A thin mist of rain was still falling, and the black night was unbroken by any signs of traffic.

Nicole considered her options. She did not dare to get back into her car, lest some shift in its precarious balance at the edge of the ditch send it sliding into the water. She could try walking back to Highway 29 in hopes of finding telephone. Her purse and cell phone were in the teetering car. Or, she could continue on foot to the Cypress Retreat, now just a few miles ahead. Or, she thought, suddenly very sleepy as the adrenaline rush faded, she could wait for a car or truck to pass, and flag it down for assistance, taking her chances with a stranger.

Nicole sat alone at the side of the road in the wet grass. A moon was peeking out from the clouds sailing overhead.

The air was cooling rapidly, now that the front had passed. In the darkness east down the highway, the headlights of an approaching vehicle flared. It was traveling slowly, and a spotlight mounted on top of what seemed to be a small truck was aimed off to the side of the road. Nicole decided to take her chances. She stood up cautiously and faced the oncoming vehicle. In a moment, she was caught in its headlights, and the spotlight rotated in her direction and then went out as the truck pulled up on the shoulder of the road opposite her own car. Anxiously, she approached the small truck. The driver rolled down his window, and looked her over.

"Are you all right, Missy?" drawled a familiar voice.

"Quinn!" Nicole exclaimed. "I'm so glad it's you! My car's almost in the ditch over there."

"So I see," Quinn said laconically, stepping out of his truck. "I suppose you'd be wanting a ride to your aunt's place."

"I sure would," said Nicole, relief flooding her.

Quinn walked over to her car. Nicole followed, beginning to shiver in the cooling night air.

"Shouldn't be much of a problem to pull it back on the road," Quinn commented. He looked at Nicole. "It's not far to your Aunt's. I'll take you there, and come back out tomorrow and tow out your car. Keys still in it?"

"It's so lucky you came along when you did,' said Nicole, climbing into the passenger seat of the small truck.

Quinn turned the truck east and headed toward the Cypress Retreat.

"Luck had very little to do with it, Missy," Quinn replied. "Your aunt sent Fred out to find me, to tell me to go look to see if anything had held you up. I guess she was right. How is it that you ended up in the ditch?" Quinn asked. "Slide off the road in the rain?"

"I swerved to miss an animal in the road. It had big read eyes and long skinny tail. It surprised me, and I lost control of the car."

"Possum," Quinn nodded. "Well, you seem to be okay."

"I think so," agreed Nicole. "I can't believe the way it happened so fast. I was just so exhausted...I've been working a lot lately...and I was so tense from driving in the storm that I just reacted. I hope my car's okay. I've been through so much lately that I don't think I could bear it if my car's damaged, too. Do you know how Aunt Jane is?" Nicole asked anxiously, turning to Quinn.

He shrugged. "Seems about the same," he replied. "I hear that Ren Steele was out your way," he remarked casually, chewing on the stem of his unlit pipe.

"He's dating my boss's business partner, Nicole said, with a bitterness that surprised her.

Quinn was silent.

Nicole felt foolish for having blurted out this self-revealing comment to Quinn. He was probably well-aware of Ren's current romantic interest, small rural areas being what they were. Nicole was essentially a stranger to the Everglades communities, connected only through her aunt. Quinn and the others who knew Ren locally no doubt were quite familiar with Ren's romantic history and his pattern of casual conquests.

Quinn slowed the truck at the Cypress Retreat's driveway entrance, and pulled up to the front door.

"I'll drop you here, Missy," he said. "Tell your aunt I'll get back with her later."

"Thank you so much, Quinn," said Nicole. "I'll always be grateful to you."

"Glad to do it," Quinn said, pulling away up the drive back to the road.

Nicole looked after him for a moment, left with a feeling that he was avoiding any prolonged contact with her. Perhaps he felt uncomfortable about Nicole having brought up the subject of Ren Steele.

Nicole knocked at the front door of the Cypress Retreat and then opened it.

"Aunt Jane?" she called.

"Is that you, Nicole? I didn't hear you pull in. I was back in the kitchen." Aunt Jane came forward, and put her arms around Nicole, holding her close in a long hug.

"How are you?" Nicole asked. "I've been so worried about you. Thank you for sending Quinn for me. I've had the most awful drive. A storm blew up and I had to drive so slowly that I thought I'd never get here. My car's in a ditch a few miles back. If you and Fred hadn't sent for Quinn, I don't know what I would have done. Now I understand why people like to keep a cell phone battery charger in their car at all times."

"But, I'm fine," she continued. "Now, what about you? I've been so worried."

"Here," said Aunt Jane, handing her a towel "You're all wet. You must be exhausted. It's a little early for a tropical storm, but the weather doesn't seem to follow the calendar. Not that the rain isn't a blessing. Why don't you take a warm shower and put on a nice robe? In case you didn't pack one, there's one hanging in the closet in your room."

"My overnight bag's still in the car in the ditch," Nicole remembered. "I guess I don't have anything but the clothes I'm wearing."

"Don't worry about your car," Aunt Jane said. "Quinn should have it hauled out in a jiffy. That's another one of his little side businesses. You just get yourself out of those wet clothes and warmed up. I'll get Fred to build a fire, and we'll have a nice cup of hot chocolate together".

Aunt Jane seemed to be brimming with tenderness and compassion for Nicole. Her eyes were dark and overflowing with sympathy and concern.

"I'm not really that worried about my car, Aunt Jane," Nicole said. Don't you worry about me, I'm fine. What I'm interested in I is how *you* are doing. You sounded so...unlike yourself on the telephone."

Again, Aunt Jane regarded Nicole with a look of deep compassion. "Like I said, we'll talk after you've gotten yourself calmer and more comfortable. Let's get you to your room and into some dry clothes." She led Nicole down the hallway to the guestroom where Nicole had stayed during her last visit.

"There's towels and shampoo and all that sort of thing in the bathroom. I'll check back with you in a little while."

She embraced Nicole, and once more, Nicole sensed empathy and concern spilling from her aunt.

"Well, okay," agreed Nicole, finally. "But then, we'll talk, right?'

"Definitely," promised her aunt.

Nicole stepped in to the shower, and let the hot spray pour down her back and shoulders. She tilted her head back, and felt the warm water soak through her hair to her scalp. She massaged the rich, creamy shampoo into a lather, giving herself some time to work her fingers around her scalp, trying to knead away the tension.

Aunt Jane did not seem very sick, Nicole reflected, but she certainly had avoided talking about herself, or giving Nicole any clue as to why she had been so urgent in her request for Nicole to come out tonight. And the way she had fussed over Nicole, and her look as she embraced her...it was almost as if Aunt Jane was able to read Nicole's sorrow and confusion, and was trying to let her know how much she cared.

Still, Nicole wondered, there had to be something more to Aunt Jane's insistence that she come to the Cypress Retreat on such short notice. Possibly, she had been diagnosed with a condition that hadn't made her look ill, yet. Nicole immediately thought of cancer.

Quickly, she got out of the shower and dried herself. She put on the robe her aunt had left for her, and towel-dried her hair. She had to confront her aunt and find out the

truth. She would refuse to allow Aunt Jane to talk about anything else until she told Nicole exactly what was going on. Nicole turned on the blow dryer, and drew her brush through her long hair. No, she thought, she couldn't let her own anxiety about what might be troubling her aunt to cause her to be rude or insensitive. Aunt Jane would tell her what was on her mind in her own way and at her own pace. After all, Nicole smiled, it wasn't as if her aunt was one to mince words.

Nicole joined her aunt in the kitchen. "Let's take our hot chocolate out here by the fire place," suggested Aunt Jane, leading Nicole out into the great room. "I don't think we'll be lighting the hearth again this season, unless some guest desperately wants a fire. Although, I don't think anyone will mention it once the heat and humidity really come in. More likely, they'll be clamoring for me to keep the air conditioning on full blast."

"So, Aunt Jane," Nicole began, "I've been so worried about you since you called. It's been all I could think about."

"Worried about me?" Her aunt raised her eyebrows in surprise. "Why would you be worried about me?"

It was Nicole's turn to look surprised. "You sounded so upset and urgent, and not quite like yourself. I guess I just assumed that something was wrong...that you were sick."

Aunt Jane snorted. "i can't afford to be sick. Not with all the work around here."

"Then, there's nothing wrong with you?"

Aunt Jane looked at Nicole sharply.

"Where did you get that idea?" she questioned.

"Like I said, I guess I just assumed that there was, from the tone of your voice when your called me, and from what you said."

Jane took a deep breath. "Well, Nicole, I'm very concerned about something, but it has nothing to do with my health, knock on wood. Would you mind if I asked you a few questions?"

"Of course not," Nicole replied, puzzled. "What about?"

"The gallery where you work. How are things going there?'

"Good, I guess."

"I mean financially, how is the business doing?"

Nicole looked at her aunt, surprised. "I don't really know. I know what I sell, and I notice, generally, what seems to be moving. There's quit a bit of art goes in and out, but a lot of it is on consignment. I don't actually have anything to do with any of the accounting. And, Marta and Allen do all the purchasing."

Her aunt nodded. "Has Allen ever said anything to your about the gallery's financial position?"

Nicole thought for a while. "We talk about publicity, and all manner of things related to promotion and sales. We've never talked about how the gallery is doing financially, and I've never seen a balance sheet. That isn't really an area of the business that I've gotten involved with. I guess I've always assumed that things were all right, since Allen has never brought up anything to the contrary. Plus, that big party we just had doesn't seem like something Allen would have had to put on if the Pelican was having financial problems."

Aunt Jane was silent for a time, and then turned to Nicole. "Forgive me for asking this if you will, but has Allen ever asked you for money?"

Nicole stared at her aunt, and then burst out laughing. "Why on earth would he do that? He knows how much he pays me, and he knows that I pretty much live from paycheck to paycheck."

"He's never said anything to you about money?"

"No, he hasn't," Nicole said firmly. "He has talked recently about me taking on a bigger role with gallery, something more like a partnership status. At first, I didn't have a clue what he meant, since I'm not yet as experienced in management as I hope to be some day, and I don't have any capital to contribute in the usual financial sense of the word 'partnership'."

"And?" pursued her aunt.

"Well." Nicole shrugged and lowered her eyes. "Then, I realized what he meant by 'partnership' was that he wants to marry me. I think."

"What did you tell him?" Aunt Jane asked the question so sharply that Nicole looked at her with surprise. "I haven't actually committed myself," she replied. "I've been thinking about it. I only came to realize that he meant to propose to me last night. Tonight, we were supposed to go out to dinner to talk some more. I was waiting for him to come pick me up when you called."

Aunt Jane looked relieve. "I was just in time, then."

Nicole looked at her aunt, but saw no traces of a smile. Her eyes grew serious as they regarded Nicole.

"You're going to be disillusioned, I'm afraid, by what I have to tell you. You're a wonderful girl, but the world is full of people who aren't so wonderful."

"Don't worry about hurting me, Aunt Jane. I've been through so much in just a few months..."

"You've had to face a lot since your mother and father died," agreed her aunt. "You've done so well, and I hate to be the bearer of bad news, but, unfortunately, the situation has come to a head."

Nicole waited for her aunt to continue. In the fireplace, the logs had almost burned down. The pile of embers beneath the grating still glowed hotly.

"Let me get to the point," Aunt Jane went on. "Allen and Marta's business is facing some serious trouble. They need come capital, and they need it badly. There are also some possible legal issues involving customs and importation of Meso-American artifacts obtained in a questionable manner."

"How do you know this?" Nicole asked simply.

"Research," retorted her haunt. "I hope your won't consider me overprotective, or, worse, meddling, but I took it upon myself since your last visit to do some questioning."

"Questioning of whom?" Nicole wondered aloud. As far as she knew, her aunt had spent the past couple of weeks here in the Everglades.

"I may have mentioned to you that I thought I knew some people up in Canada who might have known Allen? The Smythes, and a few others?"

Nicole nodded, vaguely recalling some conversation around the subject.

"Well, it turns out that it is, indeed a small world. I made a few calls, and last week, I got some most disturbing information. So, I did a little more digging, and put a few things together. I didn't want to tell you until I had it figured out. Plus, I knew you had that big party on your mind."

"Go on," Nicole encouraged.

"Well, this is going to be somewhat embarrassing," Aunt Jane said.

"I think I can handle it," replied Nicole.

"I mean, embarrassing for me. I'm going to have to tell you some things that you really shouldn't have to learn in this manner."

Nicole was quiet. So far, she had learned mainly that her aunt thought that Allen's business was in financial trouble, that he might have some legal issues to face about importing, and that her aunt had been asking questions of some people she'd met from Canada.

"How is any of this embarrassing to you?" Nicole asked finally.

"Because I was talking about private family matters involving you with people who are strangers to you."

Nicole shrugged again. "But, you're my aunt. People talk about their family with others all the time. I'm sure you didn't say anything uncomplimentary."

Jane shook her head, and sighed. "I'm really not being very good at getting this out, am I? You're totally confused, and I don't blame you. Would you like some more hot chocolate?"

Nicole shook her head.

"All right, then," continued her aunt. "Let me start at the beginning. When your parents died, they left you with a very modest inheritance, right?"

"That's right," agreed Nicole. "I used it to pay off part of my school loans, to help buy the car, and to furnish my apartment."

"Well, there's more. They had an accidental death policy, a somewhat good-sized one, that was payable to you through some kind of a trust arrangement, on, or any time after, your upcoming birthday. They wanted you to be old enough, I guess, to be able to have established yourself on your own if they died—to have had the experience of becoming independent and self-sufficient without knowing that there might be some money to fall back on."

"I had no idea," said Nicole.

"Well, I did; they made me aware of the trust arrangement. What's embarrassing about this is that I'm afraid I mentioned it in casual conversation to some guests we had here at the lodge last season."

"That's okay, Aunt Jane," replied Nicole absently. "I don't mind. I'm sure it did no harm." Nicole's thoughts were on her parents and how much she missed them.

"It almost did," insisted her aunt firmly. "Allen found out about it, apparently through those people in Canada. I could kick myself for having said anything."

"If he knew, he didn't tell me," said Nicole.

"There are, it seems, some other things that he didn't tell you, and some of them could have hurt you."

Nicole raised her eyebrows. "Such as?"

"Well, for one thing, did you know that Allen and Marta are related?"

"Related how?"

"Brother and sister."

At first, Nicole could think of nothing to say. What possible motive could they have had for concealing –or failing to mention—their relationship, she wondered aloud.

"I don't know either,," responded her aunt. "It might have just been part of a general pattern of duplicity."

"So, he wanted to marry me for my money," Nicole said thoughtfully.

"I'm sure it wasn't *just* for that," replied her aunt. "You're a wonderful girl."

"And there was some kind of trouble with the business, some questionable dealings in antiquities…."

"Smuggling I think would be the term," nodded Aunt Jane.

Nicole turned to her aunt in alarm. "I wonder if that package he had me pick up in Orlando one time at some warehouse near the airport had anything to to with that."

"Could have been that he was testing the waters—with you as bait."

Nicole felt an icy, bitter anger. She had regarded Allen as a trusted friend, and a sensitive man who she did not love romantically but whom she had not wanted to hurt or disappoint by turning down his marriage proposal. He, it seemed, had been much more calculated and cold-eyed in his "affections" than Nicole had imagined possible.

"What if I had become engaged to him before any of this was clear?" Nicole wondered aloud.

"I was afraid of that, too," said her aunt. "Not an engagement so much as maybe an elopement."

"That wouldn't have happened," responded Nicole. "If I ever get married, I wouldn't do it that way. I'd want you and Fred to be there," she smiled.

"Well, I couldn't take that chance, either, so at the last minute, just the other day, actually, I called a friend and asked him to watch over you until the big party was over and I could talk with you."

Nicole looked puzzled, and then she understood. "Ren Steele," she spat, thinking of Marta in his arms.

She sat and stared at the dying fire. The wood was almost spent, and the embers still cast off heat, but little light. Occasionally, an unburnt fragment would crackle and erupt into a yellow flame. It would burn hotly for a moment, and then the flame would diminish as the wood fragment became an ember. Aunt Jane was silent, allowing Nicole time with her thoughts.

Nicole did not ask any more about the insurance settlement money. She was warmed by the sense of being cared for by her parents in this way, and felt closer to them, somehow, even thought they were gone.

Towards Allen, she felt disillusionment and some pity. He must have been desperate to keep up a front for her, and, really, for the entire Naples art community. Had he even loved her? Nicole doubted it. She had never felt passion between them, remembering her curiously detached response to his kisses. She shrugged. Allen was a survivor. There were many wealthy widows in Naples. Perhaps the expensive party at the Mer d'Azure would pay off for him, after all.

Ren Steele was another matter. Now long had he known of Aunt Jane's concerns about Allen and the Pelican Gallery, and of Nicole's insurance settlement? It was possible that Aunt Jane had been talking with him for the past few weeks, at least. Had he known of Aunt Jane's suspicions before they had become certainties? Was all his attention to her nothing but an effort to distract her from Allen, at her Aunt's behest? Suddenly, Nicole had to know.

"Aunt Jane?" she asked quietly.

"Yes, dear?" responded her aunt solemnly.

"How long has Ren Steele known of your suspicions and concerns about Allen, if I may ask?'

"Not very long."

"How long?" Nicole pressed.

"Well. Let me think. I might have said a thing or two after your first visit out here, but it wasn't anything specific, because all I had were some doubts and questions until last week sometime."

Nicole was silent. So he hadn't known all along. Somehow, she felt better.

"Did you know that he took Marta to the party last night?" Nicole was having a hard time getting used to the idea that Marta was Allen's sister, but, the more she thought about it, the more sense it made.

"Is that what he did?"

"You didn't know?"

"No, I had no idea. I only asked him to find a way to look after you until I could talk with you this weekend."

"Well, he certainly found a way. I think he's dating her."

Her aunt looked surprised. "Why do you say that?"

"He left the party with her, and she was all over him." Nicole blushed under her aunt's amused stare.

"I wouldn't worry myself too much," her aunt said kindly. "He woke me up last night, calling to tell me that I should talk to you at once. He said you were going to marry Allen. I hardly slept a wink."

The telephone rang, and Fred, who had returned with the good news that Nicole's car was out of the ditch and safely parked at the Cypress Retreat, answered it.

"For you, Nicole," he said, coming out of the kitchen.

Nicole was surprised. She got up and went to take the call.

"Hello?" she said cautiously.

"Hello, luv. You weren't answering your cell phone. You made it safely?"

"Barely," replied Nicole "I almost went into a ditch in the rainstorm."

"Are you all right? And your car?"

"No damage, nothing serious."

"That's good news," he said brightly. "And your aunt—how is she?"

"She's okay. She was upset, not ill, like I had feared. We talked."

"Oh?"

"Yes."

"I see," Allen said finally, to break the silence. "When will you be returning to Naples?"

"I'm not sure."

"Oh. You'll be wanting a few days off from work, perhaps?"

"Allen," Nicole said, wondering how to begin, "why didn't you tell me that Marta is your sister?"

"It never came up." Nicole visualized him giving his casual shrug and charming smile.

"What was in that package you had me fly up to Orlando to pick up a few weeks ago?"

"Nothing much," he said, cautiously.

"What was it?" Nicole pursued.

"Just business," Allen side-stepped. "nothing to worry about."

"Was it an antiquity of some type?" pressed Nicole. She was becoming angry again as Allen tried to dodge her questions.

After a silence, he finally said, "I think it would be better if we didn't discuss it just now."

"Allen," Nicole persisted, her anger growing, "you've talked about us becoming partners. What type of a partner did you see me as?"

"As a full partner, a partner for life, perhaps," he replied softly. "It would be so much better if we were together, in person, having this discussion over a nice meal and a bottle of wine. If your aunt is well, can't you consider coming home tomorrow? It would be so much easier and more pleasant to talk about the future in lovely surroundings."

"Aunt Jane has told me that she has spoken to some people in Canada who know you," Nicole said.

"Ah."

Nicole waited, but Allen was too clever to tip his hand without knowing how much Nicole actually knew.

At last, he said, "I think the most important thing for you to know, regardless of what you may have heard from your aunt is how very much I love you and want you to be my wife.

We could have a wonderful life together," he continued. "We could see more of the world...travel. We could build the business together...it's just now really taking off. With your help, there would be no limit to what we could accomplish. Please come home, Nicole. I need you."

"I think, Allen," said Nicole carefully, "that what you need is my money."

From the other end of the telephone, Nicole heard a long, defeated sigh.

"Good night, Allen," she said quietly, and hung up.

Chapter 11

"How are you feeling this morning?" Aunt Jane asked Nicole over a breakfast of Spanish omelet and toast. Fred had joined them, and was drinking his second cup of Cuban coffee.

"Not too bad," replied Nicole. "i slept okay, surprisingly. I'm thinking things over."

"Understandable," nodded her aunt. "Should be a nice day, now that the front has passed over."

"They say more rain is expected tomorrow," commented Fred.

"I heard," said Jane. "Normal or above-normal rainfall predicted for the month."

"That should take care of the immediate drought problem. No more threat of fires, at least. We can all relax.'

"You still better watch your ashed when you smoke your pipe,' Jane admonished.

"Always, dear," Fred smiled. "I wouldn't thin o doing otherwise." He cast a flirtatious smile across the table a her.

Aunt Jane lowered her eyes.

"Should we tell Nicole?" Fred asked.

"Tell Nicole what?" Jane seemed a little flustered.

"You know."

"What are you two talking about?" asked Nicole, looking first at her aunt and then at Fred.

"Well, it seems Fred is about to let the cat out of the bag, so we might as well tell you," replied her aunt, looking disapprovingly at Fred.

"I've asked your aunt to marry me, and she's accepted, Nicole. Show her your ring," he said to Jane.

"Why, that's so romantic!" Nicole exclaimed, admiring the large, square-cut aquamarine that her aunt was now wearing on her left hand.

"I picked that stone up in South America a long time ago" Fred said proudly, "and I've been saying it all this time. Had it polished up and set at a shop in Naples, as a matter of fact."

"It's beautiful!"

"It's my birthstone, too," said Jane softly.

"I knew that," said Fred with a broad smile.

"You did?"

"I sue did. March."

Fred took her had and kissed it.

"The wedding's going to be here, at the Cypress, bu the honeymoon's going to be in the Bahamas."

"That's so romantic," Nicole said again. "I volunteer to take care of the Cypress Retreat while you're gone. It's not like I have a job to worry about any more," she said ruefully.

"You always have a place here," her aunt said kindly, "and until you decide what you are going to do with yourself, you might consider staying on."

"Thank you," Nicole said gratefully. "I don't think I could face going back to Naples right away."

After the breakfast dishes were put away, and Nicole had helped her aunt clean some of the guest rooms, she packed some water and mosquito repellent into her backpack, and set off on a hike in the direction of Quinn's cabin. The ground was soggy from all the rain, and Nicole was grateful that her aunt had loaned her a pair of water repellent hiking boots.

A few hundred yards down the trail, there was a fork, the one on the right leading to Quinn's' cabin and orchid farm, and the one on the left leading deeper into the swampland. Nicole decided impulsively to take the one on the left. Just a couple of hundred feet farther, she came upon a large pool of still, shallow water. Insets skimmed along the surface, and dragonflies dared just above.

Nicole knelt down on all fours on the spongy ground at the edge of the pool, and looked into the clear, still water. Tiny fish darted though stalks of aqueous plant life, and nibbled at bits of vegetation. Nicole sat back on her heels, remembering the day she had knelt by the side of the Koi pond at the Pelican Gallery and Ren had surprised her with his lunchtime visit.

Suddenly, Nicole felt very sad. She had invested so much of herself in her work. She would miss her daily routine, and the fun of helping the customers select the right pieces of art. She wondered if Millie would have any difficulty finding another job if Allen and Marta had to close the gallery because of their financial problems. No, she decided. A great receptionist like Millie should have no problem at all getting work in Naples.

Nicole made her way slowly back toward the lodge, taking time to admire the occasional flowering vine or interesting patch of ferns. What she would most like to do, she realized, would be to paint. She had note book full of sketches and drawings, which she hadn't found time to develop while she was working full time at the Pelican. Now, there were no barriers of time or money to keep her from her art work. This thought cheered Nicole considerably, and she picked up her pace. She might also be able to help promote the Cypress Retreat to artists, as her aunt had hoped.

It was also time, Nicole decided, to clear up the communication between herself and Aunt Jane. If they wee going to be living together, possibly, she couldn't be brooding silently over Ren and her growing self-awareness that her trust in Allen hadn't been her only mistake in judgment about men.

Back at the Cypress, Nicole found her aunt in the kitchen chopping okra for a stew.

"How was your walk?" asked Aunt Jane.

"Good," replied Nicole. "I've been thinking."

Aunt Jane nodded. "Would you like to talk?"

"Yes," said Nicole simply. "I don't know how it all developed, but I really haven't been entirely frank with you."

"Oh? How's that?"

Nicole took a deep breath. There could be no turning back once she started. If nothing else, the whole unhappy business with Allen had clarified for her how much she valued honesty in relationships.

"Well," she began slowly, "it's about Ren Steele. I've been confused about him for weeks now, and, finally, I've figured out how I feel about him, and it's too late."

"Oh?" Her aunt raised her eyebrows. "How do you feel about him?"

"I'm afraid," she said, taking another deep breath, "that I've fallen in love with him."

"You could do worse," commented her aunt.

"You don't understand," said Nicole, miserably. "I've done everything you could imagine to push him away. I tried to make him jealous at the party, and he ignored me and left with Marta. I understand now that he was never really interested in me—he was just helping you keep track of Allen and me until you had finished your research on Allen." Nicole's eyes filled with tears.

Unbelievably, Aunt Jane was laughing. "You poor dear," she said, coming over to give Nicole a hug. "Fred and I have been together for so long that I guess I forgot how confusing love a can be at your age. Sure, Ren was looking after you at that party, but it was more his idea than mine. Didn't I make that clear?"

Nicole blinked away her tears.

"Well, maybe not," her aunt said kindly. "But, don't fret, you two can work things out, I'm sure."

"I don't know," said Nicole doubtfully. "After the way I've behaved, I wouldn't blame him if he never spoke to me again."

"Is that an apology I hear?"

Ren Steele stood in the doorway of the kitchen, a wicked grin on his face.

Nicole stood up, shocked speechless.

Ren opened his arms to her, and she flew across the room into this embrace. When Nicole surfaced from his long, hungry kiss and opened her eyes, she saw Fred and her aunt standing together. Fred had his arm around Aunt Jane's waist.

"Do you think we should make it a double wedding, Ren?" suggested Fred.

"Sounds good to me," said Ren, smiling down at Nicole. "As long as it's soon. It feels like I've been waiting for her forever."

Nicole put her arms around Ren's neck, and gently kissed him. "Not 'forever'", she said softly. "For evermore."

Manufactured by Amazon.ca
Bolton, ON